SOPHIE'S EXILE

by Beverley Boissery

DUNDURN PRESS
TORONTO

Editor: Barry Jowett   Proofreaders: Ellen Ewart and Allison Hirst
Design: Jennifer Scott   Printer: Webcom

Library and Archives Canada Cataloguing in Publication

Boissery, Beverley, 1939-
    Sophie's exile / Beverley Boissery.

ISBN 978-1-55002-810-2

1. Penal colonies--Australia--Juvenile fiction.   2. Canada-- History--Rebellion, 1837-1838--Juvenile fiction. I. Title.

PS8603.O36S643 2008   jC813'.6   C2008-900685-2

1   2   3   4   5   12   11   10   09   08

We acknowledge the support of **The Canada Council for the Arts** and the **Ontario Arts Council** for our publishing program. We also acknowledge the financial support of the **Government of Canada** through the **Book Publishing Industry Development Program** and **The Association for the Export of Canadian Books**, and the **Government of Ontario** through the **Ontario Book Publishers Tax Credit** program, and the **Ontario Media Development Corporation**.

Care has been taken to trace the ownership of copyright material used in this book. The author and the publisher welcome any information enabling them to rectify any references or credits in subsequent editions.

J. Kirk Howard, President

Printed and bound in Canada.
Printed on recycled paper.
www.dundurn.com

Dundurn Press   Gazelle Book Services Limited   Dundurn Press
3 Church Street, Suite 500   White Cross Mills   2250 Military Road
Toronto, Ontario, Canada   High Town, Lancaster, England   Tonawanda, NY
M5E 1M2   LA1 4XS   U.S.A. 14150

SOPHIE'S EXILE

DEDICATION

To the fifty-eight men transported from Quebec to New South Wales.

A large number were guilty, as charged. Some did minor acts of rebellion, such as patrolling a village street. A few were innocent.

Michel Alary
Charles Bergevin dit (aka) Langevin
Charles-Guillaume Bouc
Louis Bourdon
Constant Buisson
Antoine Coupal dit Lareine
Jean-Marie-Léon (Léandre) Ducharme
Louis Dumouchelle
Jacques Goyette
Louis Guèrin dit Blanc Dussault
Joseph Guimond
Joseph-Jacques Hébert
Jean Laberge
Etienne Langlois

Théodore Béchard
François Bigonesse dit Beaucaire
Désiré Bourbonnais
Jean-Baptiste Bousquet
Ignace-Gabriel Chèvrefils
Louis Defailette
Joseph (Joson) Dumouchelle
David Gagnon
Joseph Goyette
François-Xavier Guertin
Jacques-David Hébert
Charles Huot
Hippolyte Lanctôt
Etienne Languedoc

Pierre Lavoie

Hubert-Drossin LeBlanc

Jacques Longtin

Joseph dit Petit Jacques Marceau

Pierre-Hector Morin

Samuel Newcomb

Joseph Paré

Pascal Pinsonnault

François-Xavier Prieur

Théophile Robert

Jérémie Rochon

Basile Roy

Joseph Roy dit Lapensée

Jean-Marie Thibert

Jean-Baptiste Trudelle

David-Drossin LeBlanc

François-Maurice Lepailleur

Moyse Longtin

Achille Morin

Benjamin Mott

André Papineau dit Montigny

Louis Pinsonnault

René Pinsonnault

François-Xavier Provost

Edouard-Pascal Rochon

Toussaint Rochon

Charles Roy dit Lapensée

Jean-Louis Thibert

François-Xavier Touchette

Louis Turcot

CHAPTER 1
AUSTRALIA, 1840

Early light softened the headlands, making them seem welcoming. As the HMS *Swiftsail* turned west, heading for a gap in the cliffs, its sails flapped, then bellied in the wind, and Sophie Mallory drummed her feet against the ship's side in sheer excitement. Without anyone telling her, she knew this had to be the entrance to Sydney Harbour. It was the end of a long journey, and she craned forward for a better look, the wind whipping through her hair, blowing it every which way.

She'd worn a bonnet when she'd first come on deck half an hour ago. It had lasted for one, two minutes at the most, before the wind lifted it high into the masts, then out to sea. She'd made a face but hadn't gone below for another hat. There was too much to see. Already on the voyage she had spotted one albatross, and several flying fishes, whales, porpoises, and dolphins. Just yesterday, one of the sailors had pointed to an island where bleached timbers stood together like sticks in a giant game of spillikins. Once it had been a ship like theirs, he informed them, but it had been shipwrecked, just two days out of Sydney.

Sophie had worried that something like that might happen to them. "Impossible," the same sailor scoffed. "It's the wrong season, the winds are wrong, and our captain is too smart." That night, as part of the evening entertainment, some sailors had been allowed into the first-class lounge to sing sea shanties, and when they sang about being wrecked, Sophie prayed for safety.

Now, it couldn't happen. Happily, she grabbed hold of the person beside her as the early sun shone gold against the cliffs. "We're almost there. Almost there."

"And not a moment too soon," a deep voice answered.

Shocked, Sophie pulled her hand back. "Sorry, Mr. Tattersall. I thought you were Luc."

"He was here, but he went to the other side. I was happy to take his place."

That was typical Luc Morriset behaviour, Sophie thought. Always having to know and see as much as he could. She turned back to Mr. Tattersall and smiled, "Don't *you* look fine."

"Fine as five pence, I am." He looked at his clothes and grinned. "I swear, I could not have worn my other clothes for one more day."

Like everyone else on ship, Mr. Tattersall had brought along "ship's clothes" for the five-month voyage from London to Sydney. In his case, however, it had been only one outfit, and it must have been ready for the scrap heap before the ship had left London. During the voyage, his clothes had deteriorated so badly that Sophie and Luc had begun to call him "Mr. All-Tatters" behind his back. This morning, however, he had dressed in his London best and would not have looked out of place making a morning call at Buckingham Palace. He had become Mr. Tattersall again.

Sophie's own Sydney clothes were laid out for her in her state room in the stern of the ship, and she thought she had at least an hour to go before changing into them. In the meantime, she'd try to learn everything she could about Sydney, New South Wales.

"Do you have friends or family meeting you?" Mr. Tattersall asked.

She bit her lip, wondering how to answer such a simple question. Her beloved Papa was already in Sydney, but there was no chance he would meet the *Swiftsail.* "No," she answered eventually. "Nobody from my family will meet us."

Mr. Tattersall frowned and looked dissatisfied with her careful answer, but before he could get another question out, a body wriggled into the space between Sophie and Mr. Tattersall. Luc was half ready for Sydney. He had dressed in his good trousers, but still wore his old jacket and cap. Even so, he looked as handsome as ever. "It's perfect," he exclaimed, his brown eyes dancing. "I feel even more excited than I did when school ended last summer."

"I'm more excited than I've ever been," Sophie told him, laughing again as the wind tossed her curls.

"Lady Theo should be out here with us. It's her adventure, as well."

Lady Theodosia Thornleigh was their guardian. Two years earlier, she had left England to marry Benjamin, Sophie's papa. Before their marriage could take place, however, she and Sophie became caught up in the rebellion in Lower Canada, and Papa had been charged with treason. Luc, although heavily involved himself, had saved Sophie. With his rebel half-brother Marc sentenced to death, Lady Theo assumed his guardianship, and later, when Papa and Marc Morriset were sent to Sydney as convicts, it made sense for the three companions to travel there to be as close to them as possible.

It should have been four. Hubert Thornleigh, the sixth Earl of Bentleigh, had objected strenuously when Lady Theo had told him her plans. It was beyond decency, he told her. A single woman could not gallivant around the world and remain "respectable" in the eyes of society. Sophie knew that Lady Theo had pointed out that her travels to date did not count as gallivanting, and she had heard Lady Theo tell the earl that she could not be blamed because a rebellion had wrecked her wedding plans. They'd argued for weeks, much to Sophie and Luc's unhappiness. Eventually, the Earl relented, just as Lady Theo had promised he would. There was a condition, however. He had just learned that one of their most distant cousins had been widowed. According to him, Cousin Mary Vickery would make an ideal companion, and the trip to Australia would help her through the first stage of widowhood. He'd even pay her wages and her fare.

"I've never met her," Lady Theo told Sophie and Luc. "But, if that's Hubert's price for his peace of mind, it's fine with me. He's probably right. The trip to Australia should take her mind off her troubles."

It had been arranged for Cousin Mary to come to London in time to board the *Swiftsail.* However, although the captain delayed his departure for a couple of hours, she did not arrive. "It's just us for the voyage," Lady Theo had said when the ship set sail. "She'll probably be on the ship after us, poor thing. Fancy going on such a long trip without knowing anyone. I'm glad we've got each other."

So, it made sense for the three of them to see their new home together, and Lady Theo should certainly be on deck. "I'll go get her," Sophie offered, and she ran down the stairs to their room. The swinging mattresses, or hammocks, had been tidied away and the ship's carpenter was unshackling the chests and boxes that had been bolted to the floor for the voyage. Their maids,

Eloise and Maggie, snatched each box as it became loose and began packing the many little knick-knacks that had made the cabin seem like home.

"You've got to come on deck," Sophie implored Lady Theo, who was busy sorting clothes into bundles. "It's so beautiful."

"I've seen beautiful before, child. I can wait."

"You haven't seen anything like this," Sophie argued, tugging at one of Lady Theo's hands. "I didn't know the world could look like this."

"Like what?"

"Magic. It's a magical world. It's green ...."

"Of course it is. It's spring," Lady Theo interrupted.

"Lady Theo! It's different. The beaches are gold-coloured. The sand's a gold-yellow. Pretty shrubs grow right down to the water's edge, and everything looks clean. The air has to be different somehow, because things in the distance are clear. It's not like London, where you can't see the end of the block sometimes. It's different," she added, repeating herself. "Please come and see, Lady Theo."

Lady Theo put one pile of clothes into one of the chests. "Well, if it's that different, I must see it," she said. "I'm sure Eloise can finish this."

Once they reached deck, it seemed that everyone on board had crowded around the rails. Sophie could hear loud exclamations from the third-class passengers on the deck below them. The second-class area was also jammed, with people pointing to various things — a fishing boat there, an island here — as the *Swiftsail* sailed sedately down the harbour. Luc appeared out of nowhere and tugged them towards the railing. "Mr. Tattersall's been helping me save space for you for ages. Make sure you thank him," he ordered.

Sophie had no trouble thanking him and turned to look at the scenery again. Houses dotted the foreshore. Some were obviously the cottages of fishermen, judging from the boats beached in front of them. Others were beautiful white villas. Gardens and shrubs encircled all of them, no matter how poor- or rich-looking they appeared. Luc pointed to one of the villas. A sloop was docked in front of it, and a line of servants appeared to be stocking its galleys. "Do you think we could afford something like that?" he asked Lady Theo.

"We'll see," she said in the way adults have of not committing themselves. "Now, look at that."

"That" was a flotilla of boats of all descriptions that suddenly buzzed the *Swiftsail* from all directions. Some were mere rowboats, others more substantial craft. People stood in them all, sometimes precariously, yelling names or holding up signs. "Harriet Delatree" read one; "James Tattersall" another.

"That's me," Mr. Tattersall said, and he abruptly left for a better vantage point.

One boat, powered by four oarsmen, seemed

particularly aggressive. A man stood in the front wearing a hat with the words *Sydney Herald* painted on it. As he passed beneath Sophie, Lady Theo, and Luc, he yelled, "Papers for sale? Any newspapers? I'll pay good money."

Luc winked at Sophie, then shouted down, "How about the *Montreal Herald?*"

"Five shillings."

"One Pound," Luc called down.

"Done."

Luc's jaw dropped about an inch before he raced off to extract a paper from the stash he had brought for his brother. Lady Theo took Sophie's elbow. "Come along, dear. It's time to get into our finery, although it will be at least another hour before we can land."

Sophie danced down the stairs to their cabin. Maggie had her brand-new Sydney clothes on a window seat. They were, of course, a London modiste's best guess for the climate of New South Wales, and Sophie imagined they'd be too hot in a month or so. Nevertheless, she was delighted to wear something new. As far as she was concerned, her *Swiftsail* clothes could be dumped overboard.

Lady Theo had other ideas. She called to Eloise and Maggie. "You can have these. There are boats below offering to buy London clothes for the tailors and dressmakers here. Get Luc's, as well, if he's changed. Emphasize who made them. They should have heard of Madame Celeste. Make sure you bargain hard, Maggie, and get a good price. You can split the money between yourselves."

The maids, overjoyed with their luck, set about finding every last item of clothing they could. After they had raced from the cabin, Lady Theo turned to Sophie. "You were right. Sydney does look magical. But don't get your hopes too high. No matter how pretty is seems, this place is a prison. Sydney, the entire colony of New South Wales. It's nothing but a prison."

Sophie's shoulders drooped. "I know. I'll be careful. I won't forget," she whispered. "Let's go back on deck. Please?"

They found almost all the passengers were in their Sydney finery, and their attention was divided between admiring each other and the passing scenery. Down below, people haggled over the old clothes, and Sophie saw Eloise gesticulating furiously. She smiled as she watched the negotiations. The man didn't have a chance; she'd put her money on Eloise and Maggie to get every last penny possible. By the time she switched her attention back to the passing sights, she realized that the ship had slowed considerably. The harbour master and the government doctor had climbed on board — to check for diseases, according to Lady Theo. They said there hadn't been any other ships for six weeks, hence the interest and frenzied activity around the *Swiftsail*. With everyone crowding the southern (or city) side of the ship, Sophie worked her way across to the northern side. Almost immediately she came back to drag Lady Theo across as well.

"Look," she said, pointing to the sky. "You're wrong. Sydney will be magical after all. It's a sign."

"It's a rainbow, Sophie. Nothing more, nothing less."

"It's a symbol of hope. We're going to love New South Wales," Sophie retorted.

"We can love it," Lady Theo said softly, "but we must still remember that it's a prison. A beautiful, magical one, perhaps. Don't ever forget that it's a prison."

"Oh, I don't think we'll have any problem forgetting that little fact," Luc said as he suddenly appeared in front of them. "Come back to the other side. We're about to tie up, but you have to see this."

Half pulling, he led them back to the southern side. By now, they could see tall, elegant buildings that could have been found in any English city. Sydney's streets looked wide and straight, not like the higgledy-piggledy mess Sophie had seen in parts of London. The dock where the ship would anchor was crowded with people wearing fashionable clothes.

"I didn't realize it would be so big," Lady Theo murmured. "It reminds me of Bristol."

"Bristol doesn't have those," Sophie told her, pointing to a group of people who held hand-painted signs high in the air.

"Bristol doesn't have these, either," Luc interjected with a hard edge to his voice. "Look!"

To the side of the crowd, a group of men came into view and Sophie gasped in horror. They wore loose-fitting clothes with arrows stamped on them. Iron shackles chained them together as they shuffled along, pulling a cart. A man watched them carefully, and in front of her incredulous gaze, he raised a whip and cracked it across one of the convicts' backs. "Oh, Papa," she whispered. "If this is what it's like, how soon can we get you out of here?"

"Don't fret, Sophie. He's far too smart to get himself forced into a chain gang," Lady Theo said staunchly.

"Maybe he doesn't have a choice," Luc said bitterly. "After all, as you keep reminding us, it's a prison."

"Luc, stop it. Marc's not there either. He can look after himself. You'll see," Lady Theo told him, putting her hand on his shoulder for a moment. "Now, let's get ourselves ready for landing. Are you going to go first in the sling-chair, or should I?" She pointed to the contraption that slung passengers from the deck and deposited them on the dock.

"I'll go first," Sophie said.

"Me? I'm going down the rope ladder," Luc announced, smiling at the thought. "See you on shore."

CHAPTER 2

After Sophie landed on the dock, she stumbled when she tried to walk. "Now I know what they mean by land legs," she laughed as she lurched again like a drunken sailor.

Lady Theo watched her efforts then took a few steps carefully. "Hurry up! I can see something that will inspire you. It's the most beautiful sight I've seen all morning. Look!"

At the end of the dock, a splendid carriage drawn by four glossy chestnuts waited patiently. A liveried coachman sat high on his box, watching them. "It's John Coachman," Sophie shouted, skipping a few steps in delight. "And there's Wynsham."

Wynsham, their butler in Montreal, was striding towards them, resplendent in a frock coat and top hat. "My lady, Miss Sophie," he greeted them after bowing formally. "What a pleasure. You've made excellent time."

"The pleasure's ours, Wynsham. It is so good to see you," Lady Theo told him. "We had begun to think the *Swiftsail* would never get here."

"Yet, it was the express ship," Wynsham replied. "My journey took a little more than seven months."

Sophie shuddered to think about seven long months spent in a ship's cramped quarters. She would have wanted to jump overboard, but Lady Theo more than understood the reason for the lengthy voyage. "I'm grateful, Wynsham," she said. "I assume all our horses are as well as these seem to be."

"John Coachman exercised them every moment he could," Wynsham answered. "Every time the ship stopped at a port, we let them run a little, and John babied them through the storms. I swear, those horses think they're his children, and that when he talks, it's only to them. I've never seen such devoted equines."

"Not even at Astley's Circus in London?" Luc asked, arriving in a rush. "It's good to see you, Wynsham."

"And you as well, Master Luc," Wynsham answered, then slipped into his major-domo role. "My lady, allow me to escort you to the carriage. I've engaged two suites at the Royal Hotel. Now, if you'll introduce me to Mrs. Vickery, we can leave."

"Unfortunately, Wynsham, Mrs. Vickery is not with us. She missed the boat in London. She must have been detained by an accident or some other calamity," Lady Theo told him.

Sophie hid her smile. Cousin Mary was a very sore topic for Lady Theo.

"I see," Wynsham replied, sounding a little bewildered. "Well then, let's get going. John will come back for Eloise and young Maggie. One thing first, though." He stopped and waited until he had Luc's attention. "It's my duty to warn you: keep your eyes open and a hand on your possessions. The pickpockets here are better than any in London. They'll steal anything that's not nailed down. And, Master Luc, you keep your eyes skinned. You never know who you'll see!"

"Papa?" Sophie broke in immediately. "Have you seen Papa?"

"Just last Sunday," Wynsham replied to her surprise. "He sends his love. Of course, none of us had a firm idea when you would arrive. It will be a happy surprise for him."

"Where is he, Wynsham? Is it easy to see him?" Lady Theo demanded as they walked towards the carriage.

"Yes and no. The best time is Sundays. I will explain it all later, at the hotel."

"But ...," Sophie began.

"Later, Sophie. Just wait a little longer," Lady Theo interrupted. "We don't want to start and then stop again when we reach the hotel. That would be even more frustrating. Now, where's Luc got to?"

Luc was already in the carriage chatting a mile a

minute with John, who then drove them to the hotel. After Wynsham settled them into their suite of rooms, he and Lady Theo had a quiet conversation. At its end, Lady Theo nodded a couple of times. "I'm afraid I have to go out immediately," she said, to Sophie's dismay. "Wynsham has an important appointment this afternoon. Seeing that I've arrived, it's best that I be there as well. Now, Sophie, promise me you won't leave the hotel. Luc, I trust you to protect her."

The Royal Hotel, on George Street near the General Post Office, was thought of as the best in Sydney. Golden sandstone columns supported its portico. Their rooms on the second storey opened onto a wide verandah overlooking the street. Sophie, however, wistfully compared it to Rascoe's in Montreal and found it lacking. By Sydney's standards the rooms were well-furnished, but she'd been used to something better.

Certainly, she was used to better views. She could see many shops belonging to linen drapers and booksellers. Her overwhelming impression, however, was of an astonishing number of taverns and stores selling alcohol. Almost directly across from her room was the Black Boy Public House, and Long's Spirit Store was next to it. In fact, if she craned her head, she could see more places for men to drink in than she'd ever seen in Montreal or London. She wondered if this was normal, and if so, how could any work get done?

"Sophie!" Luc's shout broke into her thoughts as he

rushed into her room. "Sophie! You'll never, ever, guess who I just saw!"

Sophie was not pleased. First, Lady Theo had left for an appointment. Then, while she twiddled her thumbs counting liquor stores and pubs, Luc had, apparently, been off on an adventure. "Well, if I can't guess, you'd better tell me," she told him acerbically.

"Guess!"

"You left me alone. I don't want to play guessing games. Either tell me or go away."

"Soph, sorry. Of course I didn't mean to leave you. But when I was changing my clothes, I looked out the window, and I was so excited, I just ran downstairs."

"Who was it?"

"Marc!"

"That's impossible."

"No, truly. They light bonfires when they see a ship. He knew we were arriving any day, so when he saw the smoke, he tried to find out if we'd come. He followed the carriage and waited around outside the hotel, hoping to see one of us. It was pure luck that I happened to notice him."

Sophie's mind reeled at what Luc was saying. "He's not in jail with the others?"

"Sort of. They're all together in a place called Longbottom about seven miles to the west of here. It's part farm, part jail. Anyway, Marc's got a great job — he's the messenger. He brings papers and letters into

Sydney every day. As long as he doesn't get into trouble, he can go almost anywhere."

"Is he downstairs? Can he tell me about Papa?"

"No, and yes. He's still got to wear the convict clothes with L.B. and arrows on them, so he can't eat a meal here at the hotel. People would ask too many questions. In any case, he's already started back for Longbottom. That's what the L.B. stands for."

"But what about Papa?"

"Marc thinks we might be able to see him tomorrow night. Not for certain. So don't get your hopes up. There's only a chance."

"What about Papa? What does he do?"

"He's in charge of the woodcutters. The men work from dawn to dusk. Then they're shut into their huts and not supposed to go out again until the following morning. But some have an occasional beer at an inn called the Bath Arms, directly across the road from them. So, that's Marc's idea — to meet there. He's going to talk to Mr. Mallory tonight and try to get a message to us tomorrow. We'll need to dress differently, though."

Sophie felt offended. "What's the matter with my clothes? They're brand new."

Luc rolled his eyes. "You don't want anyone to notice you, do you? You can't go into a tavern dressed as though you were calling on the governor. Use your head. Convicts will be there, and goodness knows who else. We'll need old, worn-out clothing."

"You mean like our ship clothes?" Sophie pulled a face. "Should we try to get them back?"

"We won't be able to afford them. Maggie and Eloise struck some hard bargains. No, we'll have to find a second-hand store tomorrow and hope it has something."

That made sense. Suddenly, Sophie wanted to run downstairs and start exploring the world of second-hand stores. Before she could act on the notion, there was a knock on the door, and one of the hotel's maids entered and dropped a curtsy. "There's a Mrs. Halladay downstairs to see you, Miss. She says she knows you from the boat."

Sophie looked at Luc. "Halladay? There wasn't anyone called that, was there?" Guarded by Lady Theo, she had met only the first-class passengers. Luc, however, had roamed the ship, making friends with everyone. If there had been a Mrs. Halladay, he would know her.

But he shook his head. "There was a Sam Hallett, but he wasn't married. In any case, he's only a little older than me."

"You're married, and you're fifteen," Sophie pointed out.

That was true, but, only to a certain extent. A year before Luc had married Sophie. It had been a last-ditch effort to stop her brothers from taking her away from Lady Theo and Montreal. In a desperate effort to give

Sophie a legal guardian in Montreal, the fourteen-year-old Luc had married the then-twelve-year-old Sophie.

Sophie still had no idea if her marriage was still legal. In fact, she didn't understand much about it at all. Her life hadn't changed. Luc had no say in what she did. Truth to tell, he had little say in what he did either, for Lady Theo took her guardianship seriously. What she said determined what was done. Furthermore, Sophie was still Sophie Mallory, not Sophie Morriset. It said so on all the official papers. Lastly, she and Luc were the best of friends, not like married people who seemed to argue so much of the time.

"Miss?" the maid said. "What about Mrs. Halladay? Shall I show her up?"

Luc shrugged. "What do you say, Soph? Let's find out who the lady is and what she wants from us."

Chapter 3

"Waif" was the only word to describe Mrs. Halladay, Sophie thought. She seemed only a few years older than Sophie herself. A few inches shorter, she carried herself so proudly that she looked to be the same height. Her dress, while not made of the best fabric, was beautifully tailored. Its quality showed in every seam, and Sophie wondered why anyone would pay for such exquisite sewing but third-rate fabric.

Mrs. Halladay's face looked so pinched and gaunt that Luc immediately ordered sandwiches and tea to be brought up. No matter how much she might try to hide it, she seemed on the brink of starvation.

She smiled her thanks to Luc as she walked across to Sophie. "It's very kind of you to see me, Miss Thornleigh."

Sophie looked at Luc. Now she knew that Mrs. Halladay hadn't been on the *Swiftsail,* and was certain, furthermore, that Mrs. Halladay didn't know her or Lady Theo. She wanted to ask her to leave, but curiosity took over. "You see us all at sixes and sevens," she said, pointing to the partially unpacked boxes around the room. "Why did you ask to see me?"

"I won't keep you long," Mrs. Halladay said, staring at Sophie. "I'm an honest person, I am, and it's hard to be that in this town. Hard to run an honest business, even harder to make your own way. Especially when you're an ex-convict. But, Miss Thornleigh, if you would just allow me to sketch a couple of your dresses, I'd have the latest fashions in Sydney for girls your age. Lots of modistes have good ladies' dresses, everything smack up to the nines. But I reckon that it's hard to find good, fashionable clothing for young ladies. If I could offer that, I'd get established. Get my own shop. But I need to see the latest styles. If you would just let me sketch your dresses, I could make it worth your while. Not now, though. I'll need every penny to buy the cloth. But in a month's time? Say five pounds then for five minutes now?"

Sophie wondered where Lady Theo was, and what she'd make of this very strange proposition. She was about to send Mrs. Halladay packing when something in her eyes made Sophie change her mind. "Four dresses of mine as well as the one I have on," she offered in a crisp, no-nonsense voice, "and, if my guardian's clothes have arrived, I can let you see one of hers."

"Sophie!" Luc exclaimed, sounding scandalized.

Sophie didn't understand her decision herself. Rather than face Luc, she pulled four dresses from her travelling box, then went into Lady Theo's room. When she explained her errand, Eloise, Lady Theo's personal maid, looked as horrified as Luc. "Miss Sophie? What are you doing?"

Sophie insisted, and Eloise grudgingly carried one of Lady Theo's everyday dresses into Sophie's room. While Mrs. Halladay sketched its lines, she guarded the dress as jealously as a dog might its bone, every line of her body showing the outrage she felt as this slight against Lady Theo's dignity. Sophie knew, as clearly as though Eloise had threatened it, that when Lady Theo arrived back from wherever she was, Eloise would be first in line to complain about this strange happening.

The plates of sandwiches and cakes arrived, together with a large pot of tea. Sophie made a production of pouring it for the three of them, then handed around the food. Mrs. Halladay stared at the delicate cucumber sandwiches as hungrily as the proverbial mouse eyeing a morsel of cheese. When she took one, she seemed to force herself to eat it slowly. Unobtrusively, Sophie put four more onto her plate before she helped herself. Luc took the rest and half the cakes. For a while, conversation ceased. Then Mrs. Halladay extracted a charcoal pencil and another sketchbook from her voluminous handbag and arranged one of Sophie's dresses on the bed.

While she made detailed sketches, Sophie studied her carefully. Her clothes now made sense. The sewing in them was the best possible advertisement for the proposed shop. If she had only used the best fabric, any lady in London, even young Queen Victoria, would have been proud to have worn the dress.

Luc had obviously been thinking, too, while he demolished the sandwiches and cakes. "About those five pounds you've promised us, Mrs. Halladay ...."

The seamstress glanced at him immediately, a frightened look on her face. "I can't pay more, sir."

"No, it's not that. I was wondering, though, if you would care to make a partial trade instead?"

"Miss? What's he talking about? This dress is worth every penny of fifty pounds. I couldn't take it." Mrs. Halladay looked at the dress she was drawing, and Sophie could see how much she yearned to own it.

"And I couldn't let you," Sophie answered. "What are you talking about, Luc?"

"Mrs. Halladay, we need some old, broken-in clothes that workers might wear. Ones that won't draw attention to us," he said. "I thought you might be able to get some for us. You know all our sizes and you could probably get them more easily and discreetly than we could."

"That's a brilliant idea, Luc," Sophie told him.

"I know just where I could get outfits for the three of you," Mrs. Halladay broke in eagerly. "Don't go telling me what you want them for. I don't want to know. When would you want them by?"

"This time tomorrow?"

"I'll have them here early tomorrow morning." She stopped and appeared to be calculating costs in her head. "Say, three complete outfits, no questions asked, and three pounds at the end of the month?"

"Outfits. Boots included," said Luc.

Mrs. Halladay nodded.

"Done." Sophie said decisively. "I'll talk with my guardian. Maybe you could make me a dress in a very light material for the summer. I've a feeling these are too heavy. If she approves, you could make two or three more and we'll pay you for them."

The older girl's face became radiant. "I'll use the finest Indian voile, I will." She scribbled her address on a sheet ripped from her sketchbook and took one last look at Sophie's boxes of clothes. "When you outgrow these, would you sell them to me? Or even let me sketch them? You must know our fashions are always a year or so behind London's. Some rags are worth their weight in gold."

Sophie thought back to the frenzied auction on the harbour, and the huge smiles Eloise and Maggie wore. "I'll ask Lady Thornleigh," she said, suddenly becoming wary as she wondered what Lady Theo would think of this encounter. Had she been too reckless and trusting? After all, they had no guarantee that Mrs. Halladay would come back with the second-hand clothes, or, later, with the money.

"I'll see you out," Luc said, picking up on Sophie's unease. "You can show me where your shop is. Just a moment, please."

Sophie heard him asking Eloise to keep an eye on Sophie and thought he'd come back with Mrs. Halladay's complete history. He'd probably chat with everyone he met on the way to her shop and back. He was a walking newspaper. His thirst for information was only rivalled by his knack of acquiring it.

After a half hour of tedium, Sophie was almost ready to escape Eloise's eagle eye and do her own exploring. However, she well remembered the last time she had disobeyed her guardian's instructions. She'd almost seen an execution. Still, it felt terrible to sit around with nothing to do. What was worse, her own maid, Maggie, hadn't arrived from the ship. When she asked Eloise when she might expect her, she was told, "Maggie's making sure that everything that's packed in the hold reaches us. She has to climb down, mark our chests and boxes, and wait while the customs man clears them, then make sure they're pulled out and put onto a cart. She'll be hours yet."

Just when Sophie felt like going crazy, Lady Theo returned. As Sophie had predicted earlier, Eloise met her at the top of the stairs in full outrage mode. The story of Mrs. Halladay's visit was told in excruciating detail and the indignity suffered by having her see, much less sketch, the everyday dress of Lady Theo was explained again and again. Maybe Eloise's theatrics saved Sophie from having to face the full extent of Lady Theo's anger, but what she ended up facing was bad enough, because it wasn't only that Mrs. Halladay had copied her gowns that incensed Lady Theo. The fact that Luc had wandered off again, after she had entrusted Sophie to him, only added fuel to her fury.

"When will you two ever learn?" she stormed. "I do not give orders for the sake of hearing my own voice. I tell you not to do certain things because I'm older and have seen more of this world's dangers than either of you. You must be more careful. This is not London, Sophie. Or even Montreal. We don't know where it's safe yet. We have no friends willing to help us out in dire circumstances. Your father is a convict. The lowest of the low. The fact that I'm an earl's daughter and sister to the current Earl of Bentleigh is not going to help us in certain situations. This was exactly what I needed Cousin Mary for. She would have told you it was inappropriate." She sighed and seemed to droop, as if suddenly the family's burdens were too heavy.

"I didn't go out, Lady Theo. I did obey you," Sophie tried to reassure her. When Lady Theo's eyes softened a little, she went on. "You didn't say anything about Mrs. Halladay, and I had to decide. I think, though, you would have done the same thing if you had seen her. She looks like she's only sixteen or seventeen, and starving. She's proud as well. She made a point of not finishing her last sandwich and kept insisting that she would pay us. Ask Eloise about her stitchery. Even she cannot sew as well."

"So she admitted," Lady Theo nodded. "Now, let's forget Mrs. Halladay for a while. I have some news. While Eloise gets me out of these boots and helps me change, would you order some tea and a few sandwiches? I've much to tell."

"About Papa?"

Lady Theo sighed with relief when Eloise eased one of her boots off. She fanned herself vigorously and rubbed a hand over her face. "Yes, about Benjamin. Now, Sophie, I'm tired and hot. Some tea, please?"

Sophie smiled as she left to arrange for the tea. At last she'd know something before Luc did.

CHAPTER 4

Lady Theo sipped her tea and fanned herself before speaking again. "It's so hot here, and it's only November. There's no breeze, although they do say there's usually one from the south about dusk. After that winter in Montreal, I never thought I'd wish for cold again. But, I confess, I'm getting close to it."

Sophie looked at the limp curtains. "I think we'll need new dresses for summer."

"Maybe." Lady Theo fanned herself for a few minutes. "Sophie, I didn't know Luc would go off by himself and leave you alone, particularly after you'd let a stranger into our rooms. Did you think she might be working for thieves and was looking us over?"

"She looked too hungry to be working for anyone. As well," she shrugged, "I liked her. I thought she was clever."

Lady Theo shook her head. "Sophie, your trouble is that you always think the best of everyone." She put her teacup down. "I'm sorry I was so late in coming back. The main reason is that I was able to see Benjamin."

"Papa? You saw Papa? How?"

"Wynsham arranged to look at an estate that's for rent near the prison camp. It turns out that part of it is directly opposite the camp's wharf. By God's grace, Benjamin happened to be supervising some men there. Wynsham and I walked along the beach, talking loudly, so that he couldn't miss us. After a while, a canoe came across with a message. We're to go out there tomorrow night and ..."

"Meet them at an inn called the Bath Arms," Luc finished as he walked into the room.

"Luc!" Sophie and Lady Theo exclaimed simultaneously as he grinned and scooped the rest of Lady Theo's cakes into his mouth.

Unfortunately, Luc's return reminded Lady Theo of her anger over the Mrs. Halladay incident. "That reminds me," she began in a too-soft voice. "I gave you a direct order, young man. You were not to leave Sophie. I'll speak to you later, and I hope you have an explanation that satisfies me. Otherwise, you are not to leave the hotel without my permission, and then only when supervised by Wynsham, John Coachman, or myself. You're the man of this family, Luc, and I expect you to act like one."

Sophie couldn't stand the hurt look on Luc's face. She could almost feel his pain. Luc had a good reason for accompanying Mrs. Halladay. They needed to find out if she was a trickster. He had been responsible, if only Lady Theo could see it. "That's why Luc went out," she tried to explain. "Part of the deal with Mrs. Halladay is that she supply three sets of clothes that we can wear to the Bath Arms. You don't know, but Luc met Marc. He's the Longbottom messenger and comes into the city with the camp's papers. He found out that we've arrived and waited around until he saw Luc. That's how we know about the Bath Arms. Marc says all kinds of people go there, and it's best to blend in. Our London clothes would stick out like a sore thumb and make us a target for thieves. So, you see, Lady Theo, Luc was being responsible and was looking after us."

Lady Theo's face softened a little as she listened to this long explanation. "You'll still see me later, please Luc."

Sophie gave him a look of commiseration. She hadn't seen Lady Theo this angry for a long, long time. To lighten the mood in the room, she asked, "Did you see a kangaroo? Or one of the Australian ostriches?"

"Actually, I saw a few kangaroos. They're shy. You can't get near them. I've heard there's also some in the park that's a mile or so from here. Maybe John can take you both tomorrow to see them."

"Tell us more about the house," Sophie pleaded, pleased to see Lady Theo smiling again.

"Well, there are kangaroos in its gardens."

"Oh, if only I were at school. Everyone would be so jealous," Luc interrupted, his eyes gleaming at the thought of telling his old friends about a house with kangaroos.

"Be careful what you wish for, young Luc. Finding a good school for you is high on my list of things to do."

"That will keep you busy," Sophie said, laughing at Luc's sour face.

"You too, Sophie," Lady Theo went on. "I've heard there are a couple of excellent schools for girls here."

Sophie groaned aloud. It had been such a long time since she had gone to school, and the thought of sitting quietly in a classroom, with girls she might not even like, did not appeal to her in the slightest. She had become too accustomed to adventures. "What else is on your list, Lady Theo?" she asked, hoping that the list was long, and that girls' schools were at the bottom of it.

"Tomorrow, we'll look at more houses in different parts of the city. Wynsham has whittled down the possible to five. So, I want you both to think hard and long about where you want to live. The house near Longbottom is nearly six miles out of town and we'd be isolated if we lived there. It's also in terrible condition. On the other hand, there's a house that's apparently near the one you pointed out from the ship, Luc, in a place called Double Bay. It's almost as far from the city as Longbottom, but in the opposite direction. The other three are here in the city itself. So, as I said, think hard. Talk about it amongst yourselves, and make sure you dress very respectably for dinner tonight. Wynsham predicts that half of Sydney will dine here tonight to look the new arrivals over. We need to show them who we are. Rich, prospective buyers of land."

Sophie gulped. "How about my rose dress from Madame Dubois? If I wear that," she went on with a little note of bitterness in her voice, "no one will imagine that my papa's a convict in Longbottom."

Sophie's rose dress acted as an armour that night against everyone's prying eyes. Even though Lady Theo had demanded a private parlour, it seemed they were always on display. When the door opened for a server to enter, they were always several people grouped around the doorway. Some spoke loudly, and Sophie wondered if they were trying to impress Lady Theo. The boldest opened the parlour's door "by mistake." While they apologized, the women with them ogled Sophie and Lady Theo, assessing their clothes.

One man wore three or four gaudy rings on each finger. "How can he use his hands? He can't possibly bend his fingers," Luc commented once a waiter shut the door in his face.

"He'd better not go into a boat with all those gold chains around his neck. He'd sink it," Sophie laughed.

"And, what about his feet? There was a gap of four inches between his trousers and boots."

While Luc and Sophie giggled, Lady Theo stared at her plate in silence. When the silence became uncomfortable, Luc took a long look at her face and shifted his chair so that it shielded her a little from the curious people crowding the doorway. "I know this is the last time we'll be on display at this hotel," he said. "Right, Lady T?"

Sophie didn't need to hear an answer. She simply looked at Lady Theo's face with its angry splotches of red staining her cheeks and her lips pursed into a tight line. She touched her guardian's hand gently. "Now you see why I don't want to go to school. Some of the girls we saw tonight might be in my class."

Luc choked back a laugh and hastily drank some water. Lady Theo merely quelled Sophie's hopes with a look. "As I said earlier, this week is one of choices. Now," she said, rising to her feet, "I believe I am finished."

Excited by the thought of finally seeing Papa and the choices she had to make, Sophie found it difficult to sleep. She hadn't been allowed to have a part in the decision when Lady Theo had rented the house in Montreal. That was different, though. Sophie had known it would be temporary, because, sooner or later, Papa would stand his trial. Then, she'd believed, they would either go home to Malloryville in Vermont, or maybe back to England. None of them had thought of New South Wales. Why would they? Papa was innocent. Yet, the court martial had sent him to Australia for "the term of his natural life." That meant that no matter how horrible the people in the colony seemed to be, she and Lady Theo would be there forever. She supposed that was why Lady Theo had told them to think hard about the houses. Maybe the one closest to Papa wouldn't be as bad as Lady Theo had made it sound. Maybe that would be the one she liked the best.

The next morning, John Coachman brought the carriage around with two splendid picnic baskets strapped in the luggage compartment. They headed east through the heights of Woolloomolloo where, he told them, the city's elite lived. When Sophie looked back at the city, it began to make sense to her. Spires of cathedrals and churches studded the middle, residential part and three windmills whirled lazily in the breeze. Most of the commercial activity centred around the harbour. Boats went in all directions; some powered by men, others by sail. She even saw a small paddle-wheel steamer buzzing in and out of the tall sailboats. Nearby, a large Union Jack waved high around the turrets of a castle-like building that John Coachman said was Government House, the governor's residence.

Their first stop was in Double Bay. Sophie loved the villa Wynsham had chosen. It was white and built about fifty yards from the harbour's edge. It was in a kind of bay-let (if there were such a word), and tiny promontories sloped down to the sea on either side. The garden was spectacular. Sophie had never seen some of the flowers or shrubs before — red flowers that looked exactly like bottle brushes, golden banksias, and blue berries called lilly-pillies. Delicate bright-red flowers covered a shrub called Christmas Bush.

The leasing agent bowed so low that his hair almost touched the ground. The more Lady Theo ignored him, the happier he seemed. He was obnoxious, but the house was beautiful. In her mind's eye, Sophie could see herself living in one of the bedrooms overlooking the harbour. She loved its pink-patterned wallpaper and the white gauzy curtains that danced in the breeze. The bed was made of a rich, red wood and had four posts, high enough for a mosquito net. When she went downstairs, she could see that the rooms were large enough for entertaining and that the dining room could easily fit twenty people for dinner. She followed the conscientious Lady Theo and explored the servants' quarters. They were large as well, but what Sophie liked most was that they had lots of windows for the night breezes to keep them cool. The kitchen had a huge oven and the pantries seemed enormous.

"Soph? Come here!" Luc called from outside. He then led her to the boathouse, which could hold a small yacht. "And look over there," he demanded.

"There" was an even larger house, which, the agent told them in his self-important voice, belonged to the Kendricks. When they didn't look sufficiently impressed, he went on pompously, "Lord Peter Kendricks, you know."

"I've never heard of him," Sophie told Luc as they walked to the water's edge.

"And, of course, you know every British lord, don't you?"

"Well, you were awfully rude to him," Sophie said, referring to the agent.

"Can't stand him," Luc said briefly, tossing a strand of seaweed back into the water. "But then, I'm not Miss Knows-all-the-English-nobility-because-I-used-to-live-in-London."

"And I'm not Mr. Knows-all-the-convicts-because-I-used-to-live-in-Montreal."

"Just the Canadian ones, Soph."

"How many convicts are here, Luc? Do you know?"

He shook his head. "Someone told me that half the population either *is* one or *has* been one. That's thousands and thousands and thousands. Maybe seventeen or eighteen thousand in all." They walked in silence while Luc skimmed rocks along the waves. "Let's not worry about things we can't do anything about. Marc and your papa are strong, and they're with friends. Let's talk about us. What do you think of the house?"

"It's perfect. Well, almost perfect. There's only one thing wrong with it, really."

"The agent?"

Sophie threw seaweed at him. "No, silly. It's just that it's twice as far from Longbottom as anything we could get in Sydney. I can't imagine a house like this in the city, though."

She was right, she later found out. By comparison, the city houses seemed small and cramped. The servants would have a horrible time trying to sleep in the summer as well, Sophie thought. Their attic rooms seemed airless. The best of the three was on Elizabeth Street, and it faced Hyde Park. Wynsham took particular care to point to a building almost directly opposite. "That's Sydney College."

"Only a hop, skip, and jump away, Luc," Sophie teased, but her face turned sour when Wynsham added that there was a fine seminary for young ladies in the next block.

"Well, that lets you out, Sophie. You're no lady," Luc retorted.

Sophie ignored him and began to hope that the house near Longbottom would be a good distance away from schools. But that house had too many problems for schools, or the lack of, to be thought about. Although its agent put a brave face on it, water stains from a leaky roof were obvious in all the upstairs rooms. The garden had been so badly maintained that it was difficult to tell

if there had even been one. There was an orchard with
apricot, peach, and apple trees, but, again, everything
was overgrown.

Sophie was bitterly disappointed, although she
had been able to walk to within five or six feet of a
kangaroo. Still, she reminded herself, the house would
seem a luxury to the men living opposite in the prison
camp. She ran to the water's edge and stared across the
Hen and Chicken Bay. Men worked at the Longbottom
dock, but none seemed to be Papa. Then a roughly
finished canoe set off from the dock, and a man paddled
towards her.

"Mam'zelle Sophie?"

She nodded. He beckoned her closer. "Is all right.
Tonight. Your papa says," he said with a smile. When
Luc ran down to join them, the man exploded in a
torrent of French before paddling back to the other side
of the bay.

"That's Monsieur Turcotte. He said he remembered
you from Beauharnois, but I think he was just saying that
to please you. Anyway, everything's set for tonight. Let's
hope Mrs. Halladay's come through with the clothes."

When Lady Theo called them back to the house,
Sophie looked at it with new eyes. Yes, it was in horrible
condition, and that disappointed her. She wanted it and
the Double Bay house magically switched. All of them,
even Wynsham, felt the same way, and they discussed the
pros and cons of the five houses they'd seen on their way

back to the Royal Hotel. There was no question about *where* they wanted to live: near Longbottom. There was also no question about *which* house they wanted to live in: the Double Bay one.

"It's either that or Longbottom," Luc summed up.

"Abbotsford," Wynsham corrected. "The area is called Abbotsford."

"Let's see what Papa says," Sophie contributed.

Lady Theo looked thoughtful. "I can probably negotiate so that the rent reduced to half and get most of the vital repairs paid for. The agent seemed to hint at that. But you're right, Sophie. Let's see what Benjamin says."

CHAPTER 5

Mrs. Halladay's clothes were almost perfect. Luc's threadbare jacket and patched trousers made him look like a ne'er-do-well, and Sophie's drab, greyish dress had probably been made when the Duke of Wellington battled Napoleon at Waterloo. "I think I must look like Cousin Mary," she muttered to Luc. "No colour whatever."

Lady Theo's dress had broad panels of green and gold satin, and its neckline bordered on indecently low.

"I think you'll fit right into the Bath Arms," Luc told her cheekily.

Lady Theo immediately raised the neckline by means of a lace handkerchief. She turned this way and that, swishing her skirts. "Eloise can stitch this in to make it respectable, but I'll still need heavy make-up," she said with resignation. "I might well be recognized."

Sensibly, Luc made no answer, but Sophie thought

he was hiding his laughter. "At least our cloaks will cover us up," she said.

"It's too hot for cloaks," Luc pointed out.

"That's a matter of opinion, Luc. I'd rather perspire than be recognized," Lady Theo told him.

"If we use the back stairs, no one will see us," Sophie said.

"I wouldn't put any faith in that," Luc muttered just loud enough for them to hear.

Wynsham had been in Sydney long enough to learn to take precautions. He'd hired horses and a coach from a nearby stable, and four armed men to ride alongside it. "Can't risk the carriage," he told them. "I hear there's a rough crowd at the inn some nights. You wouldn't believe the stories I've heard. They say no one's safe at night along the Parramatta Road." As he climbed into the box next to John Coachman, they saw that he and John had also dressed in dirty, old clothes as well.

The Bath Arms, exactly half way between Sydney and the former capital city of Parramatta, was a coaching inn. Vehicles of all sizes and descriptions stopped for a glass of ale or to change their horses, and that meant a continual hustle and bustle around the inn and its stables. When they arrived, their hired carriage didn't look out of place. Nor did they. Mrs. Halladay's clothes helped them blend in.

"We'll use the room at the back," Wynsham said. "It's quieter."

It was obvious that Luc wanted to explore, but Lady Theo clamped her hand on his arm. "Don't even think of leaving us, young man. We might need you."

To Sophie's surprise, Luc settled down in good grace, and a moment later, a barmaid plopped brimming glasses of ale in front of them. "Compl'ments of the owner," she told them in an almost incomprehensible Cockney accent. Sure enough, when Sophie swivelled and looked through the smoky haze towards the bar, a man waved his hand towards them.

"Sophie! Don't draw attention to us. Remember, there's only one person we want to see."

Before Sophie turned back, she noticed that she and Lady Theo seemed to be the inn's only female patrons. In the main room, a few affluent-looking gents in tailored frock coats mingled with workers in open-necked shirts and men wearing some kind of uniform. "It's so different," she commented.

Lady Theo laughed. "Yes, but it's still a beautiful country. I love the smell of the eucalyptus trees."

"Gum trees," Luc announced. "That's what everyone calls them."

"Well, I like the birds," Sophie announced. They're incredible. Red, green, blue, yellow. All on the same bird."

"I just wish they didn't wake me up so early," Luc grumbled as he glanced towards the door. "Don't look now, Lady T, but a couple of our men have come in.

It's so weird. They're wearing their convict trousers, so people must know they should be locked up, but nobody seems to care."

Sophie desperately wanted to look around and watch for her Papa. Lady Theo seemed distracted, so she took a tiny sip from her glass of ale. It was still cool, but she didn't really like the taste. And then Papa walked into their little room with a crowd of Longbottom men. They had glasses in their hands, and they made a show of looking for a place to sit. Really though, they seemed to have just come over to give shy smiles, and to make it less obvious that Papa was meeting people.

He looked thin, but tanned from working outside in the sun. He bowed to Lady Theo, then smiled at Sophie. "May I join you?"

Sophie had been warned not to show her happiness, so she simply faced the wall and smiled until she thought her cheeks would burst. Papa said a few words to Wynsham, and it was obvious that they'd met before because he clapped him on the shoulder a couple of times.

Casually, Papa included Lady Theo and Sophie in the conversation and, when he sat next to her, Sophie couldn't remember being so happy. She didn't care what Wynsham and Papa were talking about, just the sound of his voice satisfied her. Lady Theo shifted gradually until she was sitting close to him, and Sophie thought they might be holding hands under the table. For a moment she felt left out. But Papa must have realized that, for he smiled at her and said, "Sunday, sprite. Then I'll hug you so hard, you'll think your bones will break."

"Marc!" Luc exclaimed, and almost ran across the room to meet his brother. He managed to remember Lady Theo's orders not to make people notice him though, because as soon as he reached the main room, he slowed to a walk. Sophie watched him out of the corner of her eye, hoping he was as happy as she felt. When she paid attention to the conversation again, Papa was explaining Sunday.

"Although we work six days a week, we do have Sunday off. Most of the men go to mass in Parramatta."

"That's a long walk. It's seven miles," Wynsham interjected in surprise.

"Seven there, and seven long miles back," Papa agreed. "I've done it myself several times, but gone to St. John's, the Anglican cathedral. Oh, Theo, they're such good men. It's a crying shame they're locked up here, away from all their families and friends. They shouldn't be convicts. Do you know they give money to people they meet on the road who they think are poorer than they are? People here can't believe it. They've had to change their minds about them."

He took a long gulp of his beer before continuing. "It was so horrible in the beginning. People would spit at us. They really thought that somehow we'd spark a rebellion here. But now, some of those very people are our friends. How else would it be possible for us to drink in public? Everyone knows we're breaking the law, and that we should be in our huts. No one will tell on us, though. They like us."

"It sounds too good to be true," Lady Theo murmured, and Sophie agreed. It would only take one person. Just one person, then everyone would be in trouble.

"What would they do to you if they found out?"

Papa pulled a face and drank some more beer. For a moment, Sophie thought he wasn't going to answer her. But he finally said, "Some of us would be whipped. Twenty-five lashes, maybe a hundred. Or, if they were really serious, they'd send us to the treadmill in Sydney."

"What's that?"

"A big wheel. You have to keep walking in it for hours and hours until you're exhausted. I'd rather be whipped."

"I'd rather you didn't get caught. I don't want to come here again, if that could happen."

"We won't be caught. I promise. Now, tell me your news, Theo. Have you decided where to live?"

Sophie put her worries aside in her rush to tell Papa about the houses. "Papa, we saw the perfect house. It's on the prettiest bay. But," she stopped and pulled a face, "it's on the other side of Sydney."

Papa smiled indulgently at her before turning to his fiancée. "What did you think of it, Theo? Surely, it must have had at least one imperfection."

"Papa!" Sophie exclaimed, and somehow his teasing took away so much of the hardship of the last fourteen months.

"Well," Lady Theo said, her face alight with happiness, "I'd say its only defect is its location. It's more than ten miles away."

"Pooh," Papa answered inelegantly. "This place is like Vermont. Ten miles is nothing."

"I disagree. The house near here, across from your wharf, is in deplorable condition. We'd be uncomfortable, but we'd be able to catch a glimpse of you every time you came to the wharf. If we lived in Sophie's 'perfect' house, we'd have to arrange times to see you, and have you risk a whipping or the treadmill. That's a risk I won't take. So, all in all, I think we'll rent the house across the bay."

Sophie felt disappointed, although she knew it was the right decision. The Double Bay house had stolen her affections. But it wasn't important enough to risk Papa being punished.

To her surprise, Papa had another idea.

"It would be wonderful knowing that you're just across the bay. What's more, all of us could keep an eye out for you. But, what about your social life? Schools for the children? There's nothing much around here, I'm afraid."

"Pah," Luc said, suddenly appearing with Marc in tow. "I don't need to go to school."

Papa, Lady Theo, and Marc all looked at each other, then at him. "You are going to school, Luc," Marc told him, and Sophie saw Luc's shoulders sag. "The only questions are 'where' and 'which one.' There has to be at least one school good enough for you here."

For Luc, at least, the school issue was settled.

Then Papa began to talk again. "Theo, there's something you don't understand. There are three stages to being a convict. The first is imprisonment — that's the one we're in."

"For too long," Marc contributed. "Other men are locked up for only six weeks or so when they arrive. Some of the women spend only a week."

"That means," Papa went on, "we are all going to be moved, sooner or later. There are already rumours that the first of us will get out in a couple of months."

"Then what?" Lady Theo asked.

"Then we're on assignment. That means we'll be sent, or assigned, to various employers. We'll work for a small wage."

"Five shillings a week. I can make that much on a good night," Marc said in disgust and shrugged. Even if she had not known he and Luc were brothers, Sophie would have guessed they were. Luc made the identical gesture.

"Doing what?" Luc asked, and he received a look of disgust from Marc.

"Not now, not here," Marc told him after taking a

look around the inn.

Papa continued with his train of thought. "The assignment period lasts somewhere between one month or eighteen. After that, we're called ticket-of-leave men. We can choose where we want to work and who we want to work for. Unless we do something bad, that's officially how it will be for the rest of my life."

"Or until we get pardons," Marc said. "I'm not being stupid here, Ben. We get letters from home. Everyone writes that they're working for that. I don't know how long it will take, but I'll tell you this: I will not die here as a ticket-of-leave man. I'll escape if I have to. I already know how."

"Then why don't you?" Luc asked, leaning forward in his eagerness to hear Marc's answer.

"Two reasons. First, I'd never be able to get back into Canada if I did it. The closest I'd get would be New York or Vermont. As well, it would mean horrible things would happen to my friends here. They'd be locked up forever. Everything would be stricter. They wouldn't be able to slip out at night to work on their jobs. I'll wait for a while to see if the pardons come."

Lady Theo looked at Papa, who shrugged. "It does seem entirely possible that we'll be pardoned. Not yet, though. I think it may take a few more years than Marc's willing to accept."

Wynsham coughed softly. "I have a suggestion. About houses, I mean."

"Go on," Papa told him.

"I think it's possible to buy the house here for much, much less than its land value. There's the depression, so prices are low. I've spoken to the agent, and he says the owners are desperate. They're this close to bankruptcy," he told them, holding his thumb and forefinger an infinitesimal space apart. "If we repaired it, you could make a tidy profit in a few years."

Papa looked at Sophie. "That other house? The one in the bay somewhere? You say it's perfect?"

She nodded. "But I'm sure I'll learn to like the one here."

For several long moments, Papa seemed lost in thought as he finished his glass of ale. "Theo," he said eventually, "drive a hard bargain for the house Sophie likes. Sooner or later, we'll be able to live there if the rumours are true. I'd feel happier if you had such a place if I happened to be assigned goodness-knows-where in the countryside. As for this place here ...." He broke off as a couple of sharp whistles sounded outside the inn.

Marc immediately clamped a hand on Luc's shoulder in a gesture of goodbye as he leapt to his feet. "Come on, Ben. That's the signal. We've got to get back."

Papa stood and took both Sophie and Lady Theo's hands in his. "Rent the place near here if you can." He started for the door, then turned back with a wistful look on his face. "Wait a good fifteen minutes before you leave. We don't want strangers putting two and two together. Don't worry about me. I have ways to get in touch with you. Just make sure that Marc knows when you plan to move from the hotel."

Before he finished speaking, the inn's owner came over, "Police. Hurry."

Benjamin, Marc, and the other Longbottom men seemed to melt into the woodwork as they exited through a wooden door that Sophie had not previously noticed. Obviously, the owner liked and trusted them. As a group of navy-coated men swaggered into the inn, he set the drinks down at their table. "Be very careful," he whispered in heavily accented English, "these men will hurt Ben and Marc if they can. They also have eyes for women they think are defenceless." He turned to Luc. "You. Get one or two of your men from the stables. This might get ugly."

CHAPTER 6

As Sophie faced the wall and stared down at her interlocked fingers, a policeman plopped his beefy bottom next to her. "Well, well," he drawled, pinching Sophie's cheek. "What have we here?"

She jerked her face away and moved her chair so that it sat tight against Lady Theo's. When the man shifted his as well, Wynsham pulled his arm. "Mind yourself," he ordered in a rough accent Sophie had never heard him use before. "They're with me."

The policeman reacted quickly. He stood, waved to his comrades, and shouted, "Over here." Then he turned to Wynsham and sneered, "And these are with me."

Five other policemen crowded the table, slopping their drinks over Sophie and Lady Theo. "Good call, Charlie," one said as he muscled his way into the space between Lady Theo and Wynsham. "Now, ducks, let's see your teeth."

"Don't need to see yours, lovey," Charlie said as he tried to get even closer to Sophie. "I know you're prime chicken."

"Cheep, cheep, cheep," one of them chortled.

"I bet she's not cheap at all," announced Charlie, obviously pleased, and his friends laughed and pounded the table in praise of his pun.

They stopped in mid-laugh, though, as John Coachman arrived at a run with Luc and the four men he'd hired. When she'd first seen them, Sophie thought they'd looked like thugs. Now, they seemed like angels. Dirty ones, but beautiful anyway. Wynsham stood. "I told you before," he said forcefully. "These ladies are with me."

"Ladies," Charlie jeered immediately. "Ladies of the night is more like it."

"We got paid today," one told Wynsham. "I got more money than Charlie here. I'll take the young 'un."

Two of the hired men exploded into action, pushing their way, and pulling Sophie and Lady Theo to their feet. "Come along."

"Good on ya," someone yelled from the doorway.

Those words acted like red flags on the police. They slammed their tankards of beer on the table. Their hands bunched into fists, and they stood face to face with the hired men. "We'll tell you when and where you can go. We're the law round here."

"Then act like it," Wynsham retorted, standing in

front of Lady Theo.

"Try to move slowly, Soph. Follow me," Luc whispered, sidling in the direction of the door.

"Get out but leave her here, sonny," Charlie told Luc as he noticed Sophie moving. He held his fists in front of Luc's nose. "Now. Get out before your face looks like a squashed cauliflower."

The Bath Inn's owner stepped between them. "Gentlemen, gentlemen. If you're going to brawl, then brawl outside."

"Fight! Fight!" some of the onlookers shouted as they headed for the door.

They stopped when one of the frock-coated "gents" Sophie had noticed earlier walked across. "I love a good fight," he began, looking at the police. "But, sirs, can you afford another one?"

"Yeah. Remember what happened to old Lane and Gorman," someone in the crowded shouted.

To Sophie's astonishment, Charlie's face reddened, and the strength in his hand slackened. She pulled herself entirely from his grip and went to the other side of Luc. In the meantime, the frock-coated man resumed his argument. "Listen to me. If you walk outside to fight, you'll make poor Neich here," he said, pointing to the inn's owner, "send across the road asking for the Canadians. They'll come across and stop you. A report will go into Sydney, because that will be the second time in weeks they will have made you lot behave."

As he spoke, Wynsham and Luc pushed Lady Theo and Sophie towards the doorway. As soon as they reached it, several men put themselves between the women and the police, and a couple added themselves to their escort. In the background, they could hear the frock-coated man continue to argue, "Now, if Neich sends for the convicts, there'll be another trial. The convicts will give evidence against you. Again. Do you think the government wants another embarrassment like that? You'll be lucky if you get six months on the treadmill or a chain gang. Now, sit down and forget you ever saw those women. Neich, how about a round on the house."

Neich shrugged. Obviously, Sophie thought, he realized that ale for everyone would be cheaper than repairs to his inn. "On the house, it is," Neich said, walking towards the big taps connected to the kegs.

Sophie looked back into the small room. Mr. Frock Coat's words had sobered the police. Whatever had happened earlier between them and the convicts must have been a horrendous embarrassment. As they hurried towards the carriage, Wynsham muttered in his normal voice, "That was too close for comfort, my lady. In God's name, what kind of country is it when only the threat of convicts will make the police behave?"

"You learnt a good lesson here tonight, missus," one of the Sydney men said to Lady Theo. "You've got to look out for the police. They think they're so high and mighty, but they're the worst criminals in the land, if you ask me."

Just as the carriage was leaving, the man in the frock coat came out of the inn and held his hand up to stop it. "The name's Alexander Macdonald, my lady. I apologize for that incident. The police act like hooligans — on pay day, especially. I have friends amongst your Longbottom men. If you rent the house on the point, as rumour says you will, I'll be your neighbour to the south. So, I hope this encounter hasn't put you off. It's usually a very respectable neighbourhood."

Lady Theo smiled. "Well, Mr. Macdonald. Thank you for your help. I must admit, it has made me think about coming here. I'm glad to hear that tonight is an aberration."

The next morning, Lady Theo took the extraordinary step of asking Wynsham to sit with them as they finished breakfast. "I want an honest answer, Wynsham. How dangerous is that area?"

"Longbottom, my lady? In my opinion, Mr. Macdonald was quite right last night when he said that it's only dangerous when the police have money to spend. Everyone drinks like a fish here, you know. But it's just the same in some parts of London. Sensible people know the dangers and know how to avoid them."

Lady Theo listened attentively, nodding when he

spoke about London. She'd spent months every year in that city. She understood what Wynsham was saying. If they didn't go into the Bath Arms and stayed inside on pay nights, they should be perfectly safe.

"Well," she said eventually, "we won't have to go to the inn to see Mr. Mallory, will we?"

"I'd go again, if that were the only way to see Papa," Sophie said, trying to keep fear out of her voice.

"I'd go for sure to see Marc, if I couldn't see him any other way," Luc added staunchly. "Pay day or not."

"You be careful, Master Luc," Wynsham told him immediately. "You're not big enough to fight strong men yet. And those police are strong, if nothing else." Then he faced Lady Theo. "My lady, I believe you would be as safe there as here. The house at Double Bay would be the safer. I have not seen any drinking establishments near it. But if you fully staffed the Longbottom house, and built quarters for a gardening staff, I think I could guarantee your safety. Besides, think of the help we would have just across the bay."

While Luc helped himself to a second plate of eggs and fried bread, Lady Theo seemed lost in thought. Sophie sat silently, mentally saying goodbye to the house in Double Bay. Eventually Lady Theo put her teacup down. "I want you to go to Longbottom again, Wynsham. Negotiate for the house. Get a six-month lease and make sure that we'll be reimbursed for any improvements we make."

"May I go as well, Lady T? Please?" Luc begged.

"Very well. But no shenanigans. You acquitted yourself well last night. But promise me that you will not leave Wynsham's side. You are not to go off on your own and you definitely are not to try to find Marc in the prison camp. Wynsham? You're responsible for him. Do you both understand?"

They nodded agreement and left. Sophie felt left out again. "What can I do, Lady Theo? I really don't want to be cooped up here all day."

"You won't be. You and I are going to have a glorious day. We'll have as much fun as we've had in the past few years. We, my love, are going to take Eloise and Maggie to Double Bay and seriously look at the house. I want to start thinking about furnishings and curtains. I want them to go over the linen cupboards, kitchens, and servants' quarters with a fine-tooth comb because I've decided to buy it. Then, after lunch, if there's time, we'll explore some of the city's haberdashery establishments for fabrics and furnishings."

"That's wonderful," Sophie said, her face alight with excitement.

"Of course, if we have time, we'll look at a few schools," Lady Theo said in her blandest voice.

"For Luc," Sophie said hopefully.

Lady Theo laughed as she rose from the table. "You can relax. There won't be enough time today. But the day will come when you will have to choose. Don't forget that. No matter where we live, you'll have lessons from someone like a governess, or be in school. I'm ordering the carriage and picnic lunches. Make sure you are ready to leave in thirty minutes."

They returned to the hotel late in the afternoon, laughing. Their faces were slightly reddened from the sun and their hair a little windswept under their bonnets. Surprisingly, Luc and Wynsham waited for them in the parlour with an air of excitement.

"Thank goodness you're back," Luc said as soon as they entered. "Lady T, I've had the most stupendously wonderful idea. You'll never guess."

CHAPTER 7

When he described his idea, Sophie had to agree that it was stupendous. She couldn't see it working anywhere but New South Wales, but as Luc had said so many times, it was an upside-down place.

He and Wynsham had decided that it would only cost a little more to buy the house than rent it. "The agent said they are so desperate that they would much rather have fifty pounds in their hands tomorrow than six pounds each month," he began. "So, I started thinking about what Mr. Mallory said last night — about them getting out of Longbottom soon. If Marc and he leave, we won't want to live there. That means that even a six-month lease might tie us down when we might want to move. Then," he said, his eyes sparkling with excitement, "Wynsham said something, and I had this brilliant idea."

"I told Master Luc that if a person had a grubstake, the sky was the limit here."

"What's a grubstake?" Sophie asked, confused.

"Money to buy into something," Luc told her rather impatiently.

"I can see the advantage of buying the property cheaply, Luc. However, I'm having problems under-standing exactly what your idea is," Lady Theo said, lift-ing an eyebrow — a sign, usually, of disapproval.

Wynsham intervened. "The rules are so different here, my lady. Master Luc thinks we should form a partnership to purchase the property. Not with you, of course, but with your permission. You see, Eloise and Maggie did very well from the clothes you permitted them to sell from the *Swiftsail*. They could invest five pounds each in the house. I, myself, could raise ten pounds, as could John Coach-man. Master Luc says his brother has already made fifteen pounds from the jobs he does as night. If you would see your way fit to allow Master Luc to use some of his money, we could buy the house. We can do the repairs ourselves, or see if the Longbottom men can do them. Then, when the market's better, we can sell it and split the profit."

"And, I suppose, you'll charge me rent and use that money to buy materials for the repairs," Lady Theo said dryly.

Sophie had begun to understand. Luc's idea wasn't just stupendous, it was outrageous. He and Wynsham were asking Lady Theo if they could become her landlord. What's more, the rent she paid would almost certainly guarantee a big profit for them. Sophie had never heard of such a thing! Every single one of Lady Theo's very aristocratic relatives would be outraged if they knew. But then, she thought, they were already outraged by the thought that an earl's sister would marry a convict, so Lady Theo had nothing to lose.

Luc had lost his confidence and was kicking away at a tuft in the carpet. Even Wynsham looked perturbed, and Sophie wondered if he thought his job might be in danger. Finally, Lady Theo turned to Luc. "Does Marc know about this plan?"

"Yes, Lady T. We met him just after we'd talked with the agent and started talking about how much better it would be to buy the property than lease it."

"What did he say?"

"Well, first he laughed," Luc answered. Sophie could tell from his face that he still wasn't confident. "Then," Luc went on, "he said he could put in the fifteen pounds. He says he can get the other men to work on the house after dark. They all work then. They've all sorts of businesses going on."

"How do they manage that? Aren't they supposed to be locked up?"

"Not after the fight with the police," Luc said, his voice sounding happier. Sophie guessed it was because he could finally tell them some news. "The fight with the police was humongous, Marc said. You see, two of them came back to the camp after searching for bushrangers ..."

"Bushrangers?" Sophie asked.

Luc waved a hand at her, as though he didn't want to be distracted by explaining mundane facts. "They're sort of like highwaymen. Usually, they're convicts who have escaped into the bush. Anyway, these two police got drunk. One started beating his wife. She screamed for help. When Mr. Baddeley, the Longbottom command-ant, tried to stop him, the other one starting beating him up. Baddeley managed to get away. Then he came back, unlocked all the doors of the Canadians' huts, and they started fighting the police. Then, the rest of the po-lice in the camp came to help. Marc said he hadn't had as much fun in years, and the best part was that it was legal. They were only obeying orders."

Sophie and Lady Theo both laughed at the thought of prisoners being legally able to fight their guards. "And the woman?" Lady Theo asked. "Was she hurt?"

"Apparently. Marc says the way men treat women here is disgusting. All the Canadians keep saying how bad it is. They've never seen such brutality, or women being beaten so badly. Not in Canada."

"Hmmm. I need to get ready for dinner, Luc. You too, Sophie. In the meantime, I'll think about what you've asked."

Wynsham and Luc looked at each other and then at Sophie. "Do you think she'll let us?" Luc asked her.

Sophie didn't know. Lady Theo had enjoyed the story of the fight, but her face hadn't given any hint about whether or not she'd approve of their scheme. "Don't know. I do know that I'll be in trouble if I dawdle. You'd better change, as well. Make sure you look presentable. After all, you soon might be a man of property," she teased.

Wynsham still looked like he feared instant unemployment as he officiated over the dinner service. He was abrupt with the hotel's maids, and his smile was conspicuously absent. For a change, Luc pushed his food around his plate. Lady Theo ate in silence, and it was left to Sophie to try to make conversation. When the last plate was cleared away, she sighed in relief as she waited for Lady Theo to give the signal to rise from the table.

"Coffee, my lady?" Wynsham asked.

"A glass of sauterne, thank you. Have it sent to my sitting room and ask Eloise and Maggie to come as well once they've finished dinner."

The two maids looked apprehensive when Lady Theo asked if they understood there was no guarantee they would ever get their investment back. "We can do little to guard ourselves against natural disasters like fire," she explained. "Do you still want to put your money into this house?"

After they nodded, she turned to Luc. "It seems that a large part of your plan depends on the Canadians doing a lot of work. Are you sure this is possible?"

Luc smiled happily, as though he scented her approval of the scheme. "Marc says none of them do anything wrong during the day. At night, though, they do all kinds of things. Some go out in boats collecting oyster shells; they find and sell scrap timber as well. Remember the Rochons, Sophie?"

Sophie nodded. She had written letters for the three brothers in Montreal.

"Well, they make spokes for carriage wheels, and they're even working on an actual carriage. Someone else tans leather and makes shoes, another man chisels gravestones. Just about everyone has a business or way to make money. That's why Marc's so confident that they'll work on the house. They'll make money, and we'll make money."

"And Benjamin, Luc? What does he do?"

"The negotiations, Lady T. Marc says he hasn't made a bad bargain yet."

Lady Theo smiled. "That sounds like him. Now, about the house. Wynsham. Does all the land come with it?

"All ten acres, my lady, with a thousand yards fronting onto the harbour. It really is a marvellous chance. We'd be getting it at a rock-bottom price. We can't lose. It's a God-sent opportunity for us to get what Mr. Marc calls a grubstake. It will help us put something by for our old age."

Lady Theo rubbed her nose thoughtfully. "Then, who am I to stand in your way? I'll arrange for my lawyer to draw up partnership papers, as well as those for a lease. Imagine, me leasing a house from my own servants." She laughed and held up her glass of wine in a toast, "As you have pointed out several times, it is an upside-down country."

CHAPTER 8

Almost every morning for the next few weeks, Luc and Wynsham left for the Longbottom area immediately after breakfast. Sometimes Maggie went with them to supervise the scrubbing of the house. At first, Sophie felt left out and wished that she were a boy. That self-pity stopped abruptly when Lady Theo began taking her to explore Sydney's shops.

She had never before realized what an undertaking shopping was. Her previous experience had come from buying clothes and the odd Christmas present. Now, she was suddenly awhirl in a different world. They searched the haberdasheries for the right pattern for curtains, selected wallpapers to brighten the walls on the gloomy side of the Longbottom house. Lady Theo commissioned furniture for its ordinary rooms. Sophie loved Pitt Street. It reminded her in a way of Montreal. Of course, its buildings were different, and it was only fifty years old, compared to Montreal's two-hundred-odd years, but somehow its vibrancy was the same. But in Sydney, buildings nestled against each other with no rhyme or reason that she could discover, so that a bookseller might be alongside a cheesemaker, and a lawyer's office next to a shop selling oysters.

They didn't lack for entertainment, either. Although Lady Theo refused to go out in society without Cousin Mary to guarantee respectability, she saw nothing wrong in attending the plays or concerts in the hotel's saloon. What's more, she usually allowed Sophie and Luc to go with her. "There's little wrong with a Shakespeare comedy. Even Hubert couldn't grumble about that."

Sophie didn't know. The Earl of Bentleigh seemed to grumble about everything that concerned Lady Theo. But she loved going to the concerts, usually getting more enjoyment out of the crowd than the so-called entertainers. "You're too easily pleased, Sophie," Luc told her after a horrible performance. "It wasn't worth getting dressed up for."

The next day Lady Theo received a very formal invitation to the Governor's Garden Party the following week and immediately began to fuss over clothes. When she began pulling dresses out of Sophie's wardrobe, Sophie became worried.

"Why are you so concerned with my dresses? You know they're fine."

"Because the invitation's for you and Mr. Luc Moriset as well."

"Oh," Sophie said and shrugged. "But it doesn't matter, does it? You're not going, are you?"

"Of course *we* are. All three of us. We cannot refuse a governor's invitation."

"But what about Cousin Mary? Doesn't she have to go everywhere with you so that you'll be respectable?"

Lady Theo frowned. "Ordinarily, I'd say yes. But, Governor Gipps and I have friends in common. He knows Charles Grey, for instance, as well as Charles's father, Earl Grey. And, as I'm sure I'll have to beg a favour from him, sooner or later, I think I have to go."

When Luc returned from Abbotsford, he grumbled when told about it. "I'm needed at the house."

"Nonsense. As you told me yourself, you're a man of property. No, Luc, I'm afraid you must come. I only hope you haven't outgrown your suit."

"I'd rather help Wynsham. They should have finished the repairs to the stables last night. I think you should send my regrets," he protested, a look of mutiny on his face.

Lady Theo sighed as she went to sit by him. She took one his hands in hers and forced him to look at her. "Luc, listen carefully. Sir George has all our futures in his hands. He decides when Benjamin and Marc will be released from Longbottom. He can veto their potential employers. Most importantly, the land I wish to purchase must be approved by him."

That, Luc seemed to understand. Although Lady Theo had taken them to London to beg her cousin, Queen Victoria, to pardon Benjamin and Marc, she had used most of her time to interest her brother and her friends, the Ellices, in forming a partnership. The resulting company, the Terra Australis, had several investors and it intended to buy a huge tract of land. Maybe one as large as five hundred thousand acres. Its agents were already looking at possible properties. So, it was important that the Governor get a good impression of Lady Theo and her wards.

On the way to Government House, Luc grumbled continually that his clothes had been made for an English winter, not an Australian summer. He tugged at his collar so many times that Lady Theo threatened to hold both his hands. Sophie felt in her element. She wore a dress of sky-blue lawn cloth, which had been made in London for such a special occasion. It was as light as the breeze, and she felt beautiful in it. She chattered away, pointing out special shops or places of interest to Luc. For once, she knew more about a city than he did.

Lady Theo wore her best finery as well, and looked exactly like everyone's picture of an English lady: beautiful, elegant, and rich. No one making her acquaintance would guess that her fiancé was a convict.

All too soon, they joined the long line of guests waiting to be presented to Sir George and Lady Gipps.

This was a mind-numbing ordeal. Sophie felt that everyone was watching them as they shuffled along the receiving line. She and Luc were models of decorum behind Lady Theo. As she waited to make her curtsies to the governor and his wife, Sophie thought she heard Luc swearing in French just under his breath. To give herself a distraction, she discreetly looked around her, noticing that while everyone seemed dressed in their finest clothes, their idea of finest differed. A few of the ladies' dresses almost rivalled Lady Theo's. One unfortunate woman wore a dress made of heavy velvet — suitable, perhaps, in winter, but in summer it meant that she was perspiring heavily. Damp splotches showed underneath her arms and below her breasts. A few people, scrupulously clean, were dressed in faded, three-year-old fashions. Others had used their imagination, and wore a mixture of evening and churchgoing clothes. To her amazement, the man who wore four rings on each finger was front and centre in a group of other men. This day his trousers were at the right length, and he wore shoes rather than boots. But he also had managed to attach glittering spurs to them.

After a while, she became convinced that someone was watching her. Of course, she knew that hundreds of people were, but she sensed someone in particular staring at her. "We don't know anyone here, do we?" she whispered to Luc.

"Only Lady Theo, I think. Unless, of course, one of her cousins has popped up out of nowhere."

Sophie's grin was short-lived. "Someone's watching us," she said soberly. "I can feel their eyes."

Luc sighed, but before he could say more, Lady Theo took her arm. "And these are my wards. Miss Sophie Mallory and Master Luc Moriset," she said to the Governor Gipps.

Sir George smiled, and Sophie thought him quite handsome. His long sideburns were going grey, but he gave the impression of limitless energy. After his aide-de-camp whispered something to him, he turned to Luc. "I understand you were born in Montreal. Splendid city, that. Enjoyed my time there."

"And the people remember you with affection," Luc answered diplomatically.

Sir George nodded his thanks and turned to the people next in line. As they moved forward and out of the receiving line, Luc anxiously asked Lady Theo, "Do you think he knows who I actually am?"

As she led through towards a relatively secluded area of the garden, she looked thoughtful. "I would have thought not," she said slowly. "Now, I'm not sure."

Almost immediately, she was besieged with people claiming an acquaintance with her or her family. It was simply amazing how many thought they might have met her at a soirée in London, or a rout party, or a Venetian breakfast. "You're famous, Lady T," Luc told her.

"Soon to be infamous if Cousin Mary isn't on the next ship," she retorted.

Sophie saw a seat just behind them under a large Moreton Bay fig tree. "Let's sit there," she suggested to Luc, "and watch while she fights off her admirers."

The sensation of being stared at was stronger than ever, and Sophie began studying the crowd around her. A few young children ran around, playing some sort of game. Most of the adults were in clusters. The men seemed intent on talking, while the women languidly fanned themselves. Nobody seemed remotely interested in her, and yet, she had that hair-standing-on-end feeling of being watched.

Luc, she now found, had taken advantage of her day-dreaming and was walking around the gardens, speaking to goodness-knew-who. Sophie fumed. There was little she could do about it. Lady Theo hadn't forbidden him to wander off, although, in Sophie's opinion, she should have predicted it would happen. So now she sat, like the proverbial bump on a log.

When a high-pitched giggle sounded to her right, she turned curiously, then felt her jaw drop open. No wonder she'd had the feeling of being watched. Standing about fifty feet from her were two girls her own age. Ordinarily, she would have walked over to them or, at least, tried to get Lady Theo away from the crowd around her so that she could introduce Sophie to the girls.

One, the smaller of the two, was simply beautiful.

Blonde, blue-eyed, she wore a dress of apricot-coloured lawn. While Sophie watched, she listened intently to the other girl, looked over to Sophie, and laughed. Sophie felt her face become angrier. Obviously, they were talking about her. What was worse, she understood why.

The taller girl, standing so confidently those fifty feet away, was almost her exact image!

Like Sophie, her long black curls were loosely tied at her neck, rather than primped around her ears like those of the shorter girl. She was taller than Sophie, and stood with an "I don't care who you are" look. She had a slightly mischievous air about her, and ordinarily Sophie would have wanted to be her friend. However ...

Her dress was of the palest pink, but that was the only difference between it and Sophie's own dress. The pleating was the same, the cut of the skirt against the bias, identical. Only the sleeves were different. Hers were looser and, to add insult to injury, they looked as though they made the dress cooler to wear. As Sophie watched, several people complimented the girl on her dress — or so it seemed to Sophie. No one had noticed her yet. It was inevitable though, that as soon as she joined Lady Theo, they would do so. Then they would see the identical dress. That is, if the girl stayed where she was.

Rather than moving away, though, the girl began walking towards the tree. *Go away*, Sophie thought. *Stay away, and nobody will notice*. She felt terribly alone. Lady

Theo was still in the midst of a crowd of admirers. Luc was off doing whatever Luc did. She wanted to run away, but she knew that she would only be drawing attention to herself.

"You're wearing my dress," the girl announced with a grin.

Sophie looked the other way.

"It's the same, you know. Only the colour's different. Did you buy it at Madame Hallé's? Mama said she promised not to make another, but I suppose your mama must have offered so much more money that she couldn't refuse. It's too bad. We really liked her," the girl confided in a friendly way. "But if she can't keep her promises, we won't go there again. It's too bad. She had some wonderful clothes."

Sophie had no idea who Madame Hallé was, nor did she particularly care. "Please, go away. You'll only make people notice us."

"Let them. I don't care. Even though Madame Hallé broke her word to us, they are still beautiful dresses and well worth looking at."

"Well, I care. What's more, my dress did not come from Madame Hallé. It was made for me, personally, by Madame Celeste."

Sophie felt hot, tired, and embarrassed. Lady Theo had wanted her to make a good impression. Yet, here she was in the same dress as someone else at Government House. What was worse, the other girl seemed to want people to notice. "Please, go away," Sophie pleaded again. "Just leave me alone."

"Why should I? Our dresses are the best advertisement Madame Hallé could have. Yours must have come from her, because I've never heard of anyone called Madame Celeste."

"Now, that doesn't surprise me in the least," Sophie said as her temper snapped. "You've obviously never been to London. My dress came from the Maison du Celeste. In case you haven't heard, Madame Celeste is the most fashionable modiste in London, if not the entire world. She made this for me last May."

"London? You don't sound English. At least, you don't sound like other people do when they've just arrived," the girl said. "Right, Mandy?" she asked, turning towards her friend.

For Sophie, that was the last straw. After Papa had taken her to London, the girls at her school had laughed at her American accent. When she couldn't take their teasing anymore, she had copied the way they talked. Then Papa had brought her back to their home in Malloryville, Vermont, and her cousins had mocked her, saying that she spoke like an English girl. The only place she hadn't felt self-conscious about her voice was Montreal. Except, of course, when she tried to speak French there.

Her face red and her eyes bright, she glared at the two girls, then ran for Lady Theo. When there was a break in the conversation she whispered, "Can we go now? It's horrible."

Lady Theo quickly looked at her face and withdrew from the circle of people. "The Kendricks are here somewhere. They're our neighbours from Double Bay. Or rather, they will be in six months when we take possession of that house. I'd like to meet them beforehand, if I could. What's bothering you, child?"

"Oh, Lady Theo. Please, let's go."

Without asking any more questions, Lady Theo began making her farewells. "Can you see us to our carriage, sir?" she asked one of her new friends. "Then, would you mind finding my other ward and sending him home with a flea in his ear?"

Before they reached the carriage, Luc arrived at a dead run. "Oh, Lady Theo. The most exciting thing. You'll never guess who's back there.

"Later, Luc. At the hotel. Then I'll hear your news and find out why you left Sophie on her own again. Something or someone has upset her badly. You'll have explaining to do, young man. Again."

CHAPTER 9

As soon as they reached their private parlour at the hotel, Sophie burst out crying. For several moments, she buried her face in a large handkerchief and refused to answer questions. Luc touched her hand a couple of times, trying to pull the handkerchief away, but Lady Theo stopped him.

"Let her cry it all out, Luc. She'll be the better for it. Unless I miss my guess, whatever happened at the Garden Party is the tip of the iceberg. She'll tell us about it when she's good and ready. In the meantime, why don't you order up some tea?"

Sophie could hear them talking, but felt like she wasn't in the same room. When she had no more tears, she hiccupped a couple of times, then began drying her eyes. Lady Theo poured her a cup of tea and Luc took it across. "When you're ready, child. What happened?"

Sipping her tea, Sophie tried to work out what to say. She knew she had overreacted — she didn't know why. "It was that girl," she blurted out. "I hope I never see her again."

"What girl?" Lady Theo asked. "I didn't see you talking to any girl."

"Me either," Luc added. "You went to sit just behind Lady Theo, then poof. I looked up and you weren't there. What happened?"

For a few moments, Sophie concentrated on not crying. Then, she looked towards Lady Theo. "You'll understand. It was her dress."

"Her dress?"

Sophie was silent for a while, trying to put her thoughts together. "It was the same as mine. We had the same dresses. It didn't worry her. She laughed, and said she didn't care. But, Lady Theo, I know how important it was that we make a good impression. I thought everyone would be laughing at me. I thought they'd think you didn't take good care of me and let me wear any old dress. I asked her to go away so people wouldn't notice, but she couldn't be bothered. She kept asking if we'd bought the dress at Madame Hallé's."

"Mrs. Halladay's new shop," Luc told her.

"Oh, no," Sophie leaned back against her chair, and burst into sobs again as she stared at Lady Theo. "I did it to myself, didn't I? That's why you were so upset at the time. You thought something like this would happen."

Lady Theo nodded. "It was inevitable. As soon as Eloise told me that the sewing was superb, I knew she'd be a success. With her standard of needlework, all she needed were the latest London fashions. And, as you said, you gave them to her. Now, don't cry. What's done is done."

It would not have mattered what Lady Theo said. Sophie began to cry again. Luc brought out a clean handkerchief and handed it to her. "Come on, Soph," he pleaded. "I can't stand it when you cry."

"It's not the end of the world, either," soothed Lady Theo. "Sophie, you're not the first person to wear the same dress as somebody else. A cousin of mine had an even worse experience. She was invited to play with the queen when they were both about seven. Her grandmother had given her a beautiful pair of red boots for Christmas, and no matter what anyone said, she was determined to wear them. But her grandmother was Victoria's great aunt and what nobody knew was that she had given Victoria red boots as well. My cousin's reaction was almost as extreme as yours. She plopped down in a heap and wouldn't get up. Afterwards, she said she didn't want Cousin Victoria to think she had copied her. Now she's the queen's greatest friend and one of her ladies-in-waiting. So, cheer up. Maybe your story will have a happy ending."

Sophie grinned and eventually hiccupped her way to a stop. "There's one more thing, Lady Theo. It sounded like Governor Gipps knew all about us. Does everyone else know that Papa's a convict?"

"Whatever do you mean?"

"Well, the thing that made it worse was, as I was leaving, the girl with Mrs. Halladay's dress said something about convicts and their kin."

Both Luc and Lady Theo stared at her. "I don't think our situation is common knowledge. Of course, our lawyer knows everything," Lady Theo said slowly.

"Don't forget the people around Longbottom. They certainly know who we are," Luc added. "I didn't see any of them at the party, though. But then," he shrugged in his typical way, "I didn't see the girl in Mrs. Halladay's dress either."

"It's something to think about, though," Lady Theo said with a frown.

After the Governor's party, they were besieged by invitations. Some, addressed to Lady Theo exclusively, were for soirées, balls, and dinner parties. A surprising number, though, included Sophie and Luc. They were asked to picnics in the bush, cruises on the harbour, and riding parties to various locations around the city. Lady Theo refused every single one.

"I wish Cousin Mary would arrive," she grumbled, as she finished her fifth refusal one morning. "There must have been five ships come in already, after us. I can't think what's happened to her. Everyone will begin to think we're unsociable."

"We are," Sophie said as she carefully poured sand over the refusal note to dry the ink. "We only go to the shops. If I wasn't so scared of meeting that girl again, I'd hate being cooped up in this room. Luc says it will be at least another week before we can move to the Abbotsford house, though."

"Hmmm. Well, why don't you go with Wynsham to see the latest ship arrive? It will get you out of here for one afternoon, at least."

"How will I know what she looks like?"

"Oh, Wynsham has a sign with her name on it. My guess is that's she's forty or fifty. She'll be wearing grey or black, because she's in mourning. She's probably a little stout, and, of course, will be alone."

"Oh, I don't know," Sophie said, pulling a face. "She sounds dreadful. I met some women who were companions in London. They fluttered all the time."

"What do you mean?"

"Oh, they hovered around, and if they thought something might be remotely bad, they twittered."

"Well, I'm going to twitter my way out of here. I need to do some business," Lady Theo told Sophie.

The next morning she made Luc stay behind and not go with Wynsham to Abbotsford. When he pouted, she smiled. "You'll thank me eventually. I have a surprise for both of you."

"Cousin Mary?"

"You'll see."

Later, John Coachman drove them to a boatshed on the harbour. There, riding at anchor a few yards offshore, was the prettiest small yacht Sophie had ever seen. Pristine white with a bright blue trim, its reflection glittered in the water, and its sails glistened as they flapped in the slight offshore breeze. As it turned lazily, and she saw its name painted on the stern, Sophie laughed. The *Sophronia.*

"Did you name her?" she asked Lady Theo.

"No. I admit that the fact that she was already called that was the deciding factor. Even if she had been squat and ugly, I may still have bought her, just for the name."

Lady Theo then introduced them to a tanned sailor. He whipped off his cap and touched his hand to his forehead in a gesture of respect. "There you are, your ladyship. As fine as a fivepence, she is."

"It's ours? Really ours?" Luc asked.

"As soon as you can sail her by yourselves, she's yours," Lady Theo said with a wide smile on her face. "Barney here will give you lessons until both of you can handle her. We can't live on the water and not take advantage of it. Your papa's orders," she added, turning to Sophie.

Sophie was stunned. Her father had ordered this surprise for her. She'd wondered if Lady Theo had told him about the dress and her fear of meeting the other girl. Maybe this was Papa's way of cheering her up. "When can we start lessons?" she asked.

Luc, however, was looking mutinous. "I've been around water all my life," he announced. "I don't need lessons."

Lady Theo set her parasol in the sand, as though she were drawing a line in it. "Paddling a canoe on the St. Lawrence is not the same as sailing on this harbour, Luc. You have to take lessons, the same as Sophie."

Luc merely set his jaw and stared out at the *Sophronia*. "Tell you what, young sir," Barney said. "I'll go out with you. Sail around that third buoy out there and bring us back safely. Do that, and I'm sure her ladyship will agree you can sail."

Without another word, Luc jumped into the boat. Barney winked as he followed. "If he can do what I said, your ladyship, he'll be fine. There's a nasty current between here and there, and a nice crosswind."

While they watched, Luc managed to pull the anchor in. The *Sophronia* sped away, veering towards several ships waiting to berth in the harbour. Sophie could hear Luc swearing furiously. Surprisingly, Lady Theo laughed. "It's good for that boy to get his comeuppance. What on earth is he doing now?"

In a desperate effort to slow the racing boat, Luc hung onto the sail, trying to turn it in the opposite direction. "Ease off," Barney shouted, but Luc either could not or did not listen. The *Sophronia* seemed like a runaway horse, and Luc looked as though he was dragging his heels into the dirt in his efforts to stop her. Soon enough, the inevitable happened. A gust of wind filled the sail and caught Luc unaware. Lady Theo and Sophie heard a startled shout before he swung into the air and dropped into the harbour to the jeers and taunting applause from sailors on the other boats.

Barney neatly brought the *Sophronia* under control and tacked his way back for Luc. But Luc was having no more of the *Sophronia*. With grim determination, he began thrashing his way through the water towards the shore. His legs kicked furiously, sending spray into the air, and his head tossed back and forth, side to side. For all his effort, he made slow progress.

The *Sophronia* was already anchored by the time he staggered from the water. He shook the water from him like an angry dog and glared at Lady Theo and Sophie. "Don't you dare laugh."

Lady Theo smiled, while John Coachman wrapped him in a blanket. "Lessons," she said firmly. "By the end of the month, you should be able to sail from here to Abbotsford."

Sophie was ecstatic. Luc seemed so downcast, though, that she decided to cheer him up. "Ten shillings. I bet you ten shillings that I'll learn faster than you. What's more, the loser has to be the passenger when we sail her to Abbotsford."

As she knew it would, the challenge of a bet worked.

Luc's eyes lit up. "Ten shillings? Ten whole shillings to spend on whatever I want? Done. I'll think of you when I spend it, Sophie."

After a hearty lunch, Luc was full of energy again. Lady Theo sent him on a couple of errands but it seemed only minutes before he burst into the room again. "Lady Theo, you'll never guess."

Lady Theo knew too much to play Luc's games. "Just tell me."

To Sophie's surprise, Luc began beckoning a woman she'd never seen into the room. His eyes danced with laughter, and Sophie knew he had a surprise. "Lady Theo," he said in his most formal way, "may I present your cousin, Mrs. Mary Vickery."

Sophie gasped. Cousin Mary? The Cousin Mary who was supposed to be a drab, colourless woman who would fade into the background while giving respectability to their household? Mrs. Mary Vickery was young, spectacularly beautiful, and dressed in clothes that rivalled Lady Theo's. Someone had made a mistake. A huge mistake.

CHAPTER 10

Lady Theo sent Luc, still with his unholy glint of amusement in his eyes, for tea. While Cousin Mary freshened up, she told Eloise and Maggie to pack everything. "We'll move to Abbotsford tomorrow," she told them. "I don't care what shape the house is in. We'll make do somehow."

"Why? What's the rush?"

"Oh, child. That woman in this hotel?" Lady Theo threw up her hands.

"It's better than the Bath Arms," Sophie reminded her.

"I'll take my chances. What ...," she broke off as Cousin Mary returned. After she had made herself comfortable, Lady Theo turned to her. "I don't believe a ship arrived from England today. Wynsham, my man of affairs, has been checking with the harbour master very conscientiously and looking for you on every ship. Did one arrive, and we were not aware of it?"

"La, no, Cousin Theodosia," Cousin Mary said in a little-girl voice. "My ship arrived two weeks ago. I met the nicest people on it: the Simpsons from Hereford. They asked me to get my land legs at their estate out near Penrith."

"It did not occur to you to send a note explaining this?"

Cousin Mary laughed again and looked appraisingly at Luc when he walked back into the room. "No," she said, turning her head towards Lady Theo eventually. "Why should it have? You didn't know when I would arrive, so I knew you wouldn't miss me."

Lady Theo pursed her lips. Somehow, Sophie knew that Theo's cousin baffled her. Luc, though, seemed to have her measure. "You seem to have surprisingly little luggage for someone coming to a new country."

Cousin Mary flashed her dimples at him. "La, sir. You know how it is. I didn't want to bring my dowdy clothes with me to begin my new life. I managed to buy a few items in London while I waited for the ship and left my widow's weeds behind. In any case, I'm out of mourning now."

Sophie wondered if she had ever mourned for the husband who had died. She also wondered why Cousin Mary had been so eager to accept the position of companion. She didn't seem to lack for money, as far as Sophie could see.

By dinner time the next day, the move to Abbotsford was complete. Afterwards Luc and Sophie sat on the beach facing Longbottom and talked about Cousin Mary. "Lady Theo doesn't like her," Sophie began.

"Whether or not she likes her is the least of Lady T's worries. That woman is a disaster."

"She's very beautiful," Sophie pointed out, waving to a couple of Longbottom men paddling past them in a canoe.

"She's too beautiful. I've a feeling she's going to be more trouble than she's worth."

"But what can Lady Theo do? She can't send her back, can she?"

Luc looked puzzled and shook his head. "If she were my cousin, I'd marry her off as fast as I could. I wouldn't worry about having her give us respectability." He trailed his fingers in the water and leaned back. "Oh, this is the life, Soph. No snow, water that doesn't freeze. Every day when the sun shines, I somehow feel better."

Sophie did, too. Finally, after months on the go, she was going to have a home, although it might only be for a few months. But it felt more secure than a hotel room, no matter how elegant it had been. The next morning, Lady Theo began establishing a routine. Luc worked on "beautifying" his estate — repairing the fencing, painting it white, building a dock on the bay side of the property, whatever was needed. John Coachman assumed responsibility for bringing the stables up to his level of satisfaction and training the stable boys he had hired. Wynsham supervised improvements within the house and took responsibility for the gardeners. Lady Theo consulted with their new cook each morning, planning the meals. Afterwards, she and an increasingly reluctant Cousin Mary made social calls on various ladies in the neighbourhood.

During this time, Sophie puttered about. As Lady Theo wouldn't allow her to sail by herself, Papa made arrangements for her to use one of the convicts' canoes. "We're not supposed to have them," he explained one evening as he sat on Luc's new dock between her and Lady Theo. "However, the Beauharnois men made three or four for their oyster-shell business. You and Luc can use this one during the daytime, but you must always leave it here. Don't bring it back to our wharf in case Mr. Baddeley sees you."

"Who's Mr. Baddeley? A bogeyman?"

"Actually, he is, sprite. The first part of his name tells you all about him. He's bad. But he's also in charge of us. He can decide if we're to be whipped, or sent out on chain gangs, or to the treadmill. But we're too valuable to do that, I think. He's making a fortune off us. He has us doing more jobs for him and his friends than for the government."

"Marc says he's half mad," Luc chipped in from further down the dock. "Marc says Baddeley tells him to do the strangest things. Then, when they're done, he's forgotten he ordered them. So, Marc buys things and tells Baddeley that he must have forgotten ordering them. Like food. Marc says Baddeley has some sort of deal about their food and he's stealing the government blind."

Papa looked grim. "Marc's quite right. "The government pays for good food, but Baddeley sells it to his friends. They give him vile stuff in exchange. The meat's so bad we can't eat it or we'd be sick. Our flour has weevils in it. The men joke that the weevils are supposed to be our meat ration, but it's really not a joking matter."

"Then why joke?" Sophie asked. "Why don't they tell people about it?"

"When things are bad, Sophie, joking about them helps you get through them. But some of the men are getting very sick. They don't get enough good food. That's why everyone's working so hard when it's dark. We've got to earn money to feed ourselves. Baddeley doesn't care if we're hungry."

"Would you like me to do something, Benjamin?" Lady Theo asked. "I could try to talk to Governor Gipps. Maybe he could replace this Baddeley."

To Sophie's surprise, Papa shook his head. "No. Better the devil you know than the one you don't. Apparently, they're all the same. No, you keep giving us whatever food you can spare and I'll share it with those in my hut. It's too bad we can't feed everyone."

"Will anyone die, Papa?"

Somewhat to her surprise, he took his time answering. "Maybe," he said eventually. "Maybe one of them will give up the fight. Some are so lonely. Everything they care about is left behind in Canada. We can only get mail about every six weeks and it really bothers the men that Baddeley reads the letters from their wives before he allows them to have them. Then, of course, he reads their replies. Someone told me that he only has the job because he understands French."

"But most of them can't write," Sophie interjected, remembering the hours she had spent writing letters in the Montreal jail.

"They pay others to write for them. Several of them are even paying for daily journals to be kept so, when they get home again, they can remember exactly what went on. But I have to go back now. There's Thibert coming to get me."

Sophie hugged her papa and heard Lady Theo say softly, "So soon, Benjamin? We haven't had a chance to talk. I want your advice about Mary."

"I'll try to get across tomorrow," Papa told her.

Sophie never found out what her papa told Lady Theo, but over the next few days she felt a kind of weight lifted from her. It took a while before she realized that Lady Theo was genuinely puzzled by her cousin and spent a lot of time watching her. She gave her things to do, and Sophie and Luc thought they were little tests.

"Have you noticed what happens when Cousin Mary's given a shopping list?" Sophie asked Luc one afternoon as they sailed in the *Sophronia*.

"I know she comes and asks me how they say certain words here," he replied, nudging the rudder so that the boat avoided a floating log.

"She asks everyone," Sophie replied. "Never the same word. Different ones, until she's gone through everything on the list."

"That's strange," Luc replied, concentrating as he began a series of manoeuvres to get around a large ship anchored in the river of the harbour.

"It's more than strange. I think she can't read."

"She has to. She would have had a governess or gone to school. Everyone does in Lady T's family. She told me so in Montreal when we fought about going to school. Are you going to tell Lady Theo?"

Sophie shrugged. She didn't know for sure, so it was useless to say anything at the moment. She dangled her fingers in the water and changed the subject. "You know, I really envy you being able to swim in the bay. The best I can do in sit in the shallows and splash water all over myself."

"They have bathing boxes for women in Sydney. You can pay three pence, or something, and go into them. You can take your dress off, then swim in your shift or ...," Luc grinned as he looked over to Sophie, "even, nothing at all. They're private, so no one would see."

"Are you sure?"

Luc nodded. "I've seen them. Not inside, of course."

"Could we build one here? Maybe in that little bay where you swim?"

"Don't know. Maybe Lady Theo would allow it by Double Bay. It's probably safer there."

"You mean, further away from the Parramatta Road?"

"I mean further away from Baddeley, the police, and the Parramatta Road."

The idea of being able to splash around, half-dressed, when it was boiling hot appealed to Sophie. "I hate being hot," she grumbled. "It's the very worst thing about New South Wales."

"I think it's the flies and the mosquitoes," Luc answered. "I don't mind the heat."

"That's because you're only half-dressed," Sophie pointed out. Luc had taken a pair of scissors to his clothes. His pant legs reached only to his knees now, and his shirts had almost no sleeves. When Lady Theo wasn't around, he even wore them unbuttoned. Sophie was deeply jealous. The most she could do was take her stockings off.

After they returned, Sophie began watching Cousin Mary with some of the same intensity that Lady Theo showed. She quickly worked out how she afforded such wonderful clothes — she made most of them herself. She had the knack of copying a pattern, or a dress she saw someone in, and subtly altering it and making it original. Even Lady Theo hadn't caught on to that yet, Sophie thought. She wondered what would happen when she realized that the dress Cousin Mary was working on was a copy of her most expensive one. Altered, of course, but if she looked closely, she would recognize it.

The more she watched, the more puzzled Sophie became. Cousin Mary had taken over many of the shopping chores. She had a good eye for colour and design, so Lady Theo trusted her to buy fabric for new curtains, for instance. Every time she was given a list, though, Cousin Mary went through her routine of asking how certain things were pronounced. *What a memory*, Sophie thought. She never asked about a word more than once, and she always came home from her shopping expeditions with everything Lady Theo had asked for. *I'd swear that she can't read, though*, Sophie told herself. *I wonder what will happen when Lady Theo figures that out!*

Some mornings, when Maggie could be spared, Sophie walked down to the Parramatta Road, and along to the Longbottom gate, taking a basket of food to give to Maurice Lepailleur, the gatekeeper.

With little real work to do, Maurice was eager to talk. He told her of the goings and comings along the road, and confided news about his family. The heavy cost of his participation in the rebellion worried him. A kind priest, living almost two hundred miles away, had taken care of his two small boys. His wife, Domitile, was paying a heavy price of her own for Maurice's part in the rebellion. At times, she felt that her boys were as far away from her as they were from their father. Before the rebellion, she had lived in a grand stone house with a couple of servants, but the government had confiscated it and Domitile now did rough housework just to survive.

"I keep my diary," Maurice told Sophie. "Every day. If the people at home can't get a pardon for us, I'll send money for Domitile to come here with the boys. Then, at night, when they're in bed, I'll read to her, and she'll know about my adventures in this country."

Sophie looked in his eyes and knew he'd do whatever it took to be reunited with his family. As she walked home with Maggie trailing behind her, she realized that was the reason the Canadians worked so hard and took so many risks. Obviously, they used some money to buy food, but they saved most of it for reunions with their families, either in Canada or New South Wales.

None had been as rich as Lady Theo. Even if they had enough money to pay for their voyage and to live on once they'd reached New South Wales, they were part of huge families. Papa had told her that one man had twelve children and fifty-some grandchildren. It would have been extremely difficult for his wife to pack up everything and leave at a moment's notice. Moreover, they believed the government wouldn't make the men stay away from Canada forever. According to Maurice Lepailleur, the priests at home spoke of "les exiles" every Sunday in the churches, reminding everyone that they had to work to get them pardoned and brought home.

Afternoons were special times for Sophie. Usually she and Luc explored the harbour in the *Sophronia,* but she also made afternoon calls. According to Cousin Mary, the women of Sydney were fashion crazy. Therefore, Maggie had to keep track of which dress Sophie wore where. Sometimes it looked like Lady Theo single-handedly kept Mrs. Halladay's Salle de Hallé in business because she ordered new dresses and underclothes every third or fourth week.

At other times, Sophie took the canoe out. Occasionally, she simply checked the crab traps and fish lines. More frequently, she played games with the river. She loved turning the canoe and shooting it into the wake of a passing boat. When the tide was racing out, she sometimes paddled against it, becoming a little stronger and faster each time. On windy days she imagined that the waves were in a competition with each other, fighting to see which could reach higher than the others on the stone wall along the harbour side of their property. At low tide, she paddled to a cove that had honeycombed rocks and spent hours studying life in the rock pools.

At the back of her mind, Sophie knew that this time at Abbotsford was special. Strange though it might seem, although Papa was in prison, she saw as much of him as she always had. Back in Vermont, he'd been busy with work. Now, he was just across the bay, five minutes away at most. This would change when Papa was assigned, and every night she prayed that Lady Theo would be able to get him assigned to them.

As well, she gradually came to realize that she was missing something. Occasionally, when Luc was being stupid or doing things with his brother, she wished she had a friend who was a girl. There were some things neither Lady Theo nor Luc could understand and so, when Lady Theo began talking about schools again, Sophie thought it might be a good idea.

Christmas was very quiet and very different. There was no snow, of course. In fact, the day was so hot that, after they returned from church, she went down to the harbour and sat in the shallow water. Later, after a huge dinner, Sophie felt she could never eat another mouthful of food. She had sampled roasts of all descriptions, oysters on the shell, oysters with a sharp cheese melted over them, lobsters with a mornay sauce, three or four different types of fish, vegetables fresh from their garden, and Christmas pudding stuffed with threepences and sixpences and served with the traditional sauce. The day following this feast was special as well: Boxing Day — a day off for all Lady Theo's servants, from Wynsham to the lowliest garden boy. Cook prepared a special feast for them as well, and when Sophie went to the pantry for trays of food, she heard them laughing and celebrating.

A couple of weeks later, she still smiled when she remembered Christmas. It had been so different. Yet, it was the nicest she could remember, she thought. One night, unable to sleep, she stared at the sky outside her window. Papa, who had learnt the names of the stars in this new sky, had pointed out the Southern Cross to her. She tried to remember what the stars had looked like in the northern hemisphere, but couldn't. She didn't know why. Maybe she had never cared enough about them to memorize the constellations. She was just drifting off to sleep when she heard a frenzied pounding on the front door. As she jumped out of bed and reached for her robe, she remembered the night in Beauharnois two years previously when she'd woken to a similar noise. Then, it had been rebels at the door. *Who*, she wondered as she pushed her feet into shoes, *could be pounding so furiously on the door?* She heard Lady Theo's door open, Luc's voice, and a confusion of noise as the servants arrived. Holding Lady Theo's hand, she was halfway down the stairs when Wynsham opened the door.

CHAPTER 11

A young Canadian burst through the door, dripping wet — from his black hair to the boots on his feet. He looked around the group of people, found Luc, and burst into a spate of frenzied French. When he finished, he ran back into the blackness of night.

"Luc, what's happening?" Lady Theo demanded, as she tied her wrap more tightly.

"I'm not sure I understand, Lady T. He said the men were somewhere where they should not have been when they found a boy floating near some rocks. He's badly injured. Mr. Mallory told them to bring him here and sent young Bourbonnais to warn us. They should be here at any moment."

Lady Theo pushed up her sleeves, as though she was readying herself for action, and began issuing orders. "Right. We'll put him in the blue parlour. Wynsham, get lots of water boiling. Luc, run for John Coachman. He knows about injuries and what to do for them. Sophie and Eloise, find boxes of bandages and our medicines. Someone cover the sofa. Where's Mary? Maybe she can do that. Anyway, let's hurry."

Within minutes, everything was ready. Wynsham lit the outdoor lamps so that the path from the bay was easy to see. Cook added wood to the kitchen stove and put kettles of water on it. Lady Theo and Sophie snatched a chance to change into more respectable clothes, and they had just come downstairs again when a small party of men came up the path.

Papa entered first. "Where should we take him?"

Lady Theo led the way to the parlour. "It's the best we could do. The sofa here is large enough for a bed. Is he badly hurt?"

Papa nodded. "His face is so covered with blood, it's hard to see what's wrong, exactly. It looks like he's been savagely attacked. We know one thing, though. He's broken his leg pretty badly." He looked around and sighed with relief when he saw John Coachman. "You'll need splints, John. He's about Luc's size. Do you have any?"

John Coachman, standing awkwardly near one of Lady Theo's beloved Sheraton chairs, looked relieved at the thought of being useful. "I've got some boards we can use. I'll just go and get them."

He ran from the room, leaving the door open. Sophie heard men grunting in the hallway, then Wynsham telling them to be careful. Whether he worried more about the boy or Lady Theo's furniture, she couldn't tell. But she was glad of Papa's warning when she saw the boy's face. As he'd said, it was hard to even tell what the boy looked like, his face was that bloody.

Once they'd settled him on a sofa, the Canadians nodded and quickly left. Papa looked across at Lady Theo. "I have to go as well. If Baddeley hears this commotion and finds us missing, there'll be the dickens to pay. He'd love nothing better than a chance to use the cat-o-nine-tails on us."

Sophie shuddered at the thought of him being whipped. The cat-o-nine-tails had nine pieces of leather with little pellets of lead tied into them. When it lashed someone's naked back, the pellets ripped the skin and made the punishment infinitely worse than an ordinary whipping. It was barbaric. She hoped she'd never see anyone flogged like that.

Once Papa had said goodbye, Lady Theo took a towel, soaked it in some hot water, and gently washed the boy's face. Sophie soaked another towel and held it ready. As Lady Theo took it, she said, "Well, here's a bit of good news. He's not hurt as badly as I feared. The cut on his forehead's the worst. If we clean him up, put a bandage and some ointment on, it should be fine. What about his leg, John?"

"It's like Mr. Mallory said. I can set it, but he won't be able to use it for weeks. I can keep him in the stables, if you'd like."

Lady Theo studied the boy and turned to Luc. "What do you make of him?"

The boy in question began muttering and tried to stand. John Coachman immediately clamped his arm around him. "There, young sir. You just be still."

When the boy tried to fight him off, Lady Theo put her hand on his head. "Listen," she said, gently smoothing his blond hair back. "You're safe. Our men rescued you. You're hurt, but we'll get you right. Just be quiet."

"Mama," the boy said. "Send for Mama. She'll know what to do."

"Where is she? Do you live near here?"

The questions seemed to make the boy desperate. He thrashed around and tried to get up. "Wahmurra," he muttered. "Wahmurra. Got to get home. Got to."

"Wahmurra? That's your home? Wahmurra?"

"Mama's depending on me. I've got to get there."

Lady Theo looked across the room to Wynsham. "Do you know what he's talking about? Have you heard of a place called Wahmurra?"

As Wynsham shook his head, John Coachman returned with the the under-groom and the splints. After he helped carry them across the room, Wynsham turned to Lady Theo. "There's little you or Miss Sophie can do now, my lady. It's going to hurt like the blazes, and you don't want to watch. We'll give him some whisky, then John will set the bone. I think he'll pass out and not wake again until morning. John or one of the stable boys will sit with him. With your permission, of course."

"I'll do it," Luc volunteered. "Sit with him, that is. Might as well do something useful."

Lady Theo nodded. "Fine, though I'd prefer it if John stayed as well. Now, promise to wake me if you need help." She bent and put her hand on the boy's head again. "Can you hear us? Can you tell us your name?"

"Billy. Billy Kendricks. Please, help me. I've got to get home. It's life or death."

"Billy, you've been hurt very badly. You have to let John set your leg and then you need to get some sleep. We'll talk tomorrow about getting you on your way. Understand?"

Billy looked around the room as though he were trying to find something that was familiar. Finally, he collapsed back against the sofa's cushions. "My horse. Did they find my horse?"

John Coachman walked across, suddenly business-like. "No one said anything about a horse, young sir. Now, you drink this and we'll have you comfortable before you can say Billy Whittle. Drink up, now." After he had managed to get a full glass of whisky down the protesting Billy, he turned once more to Lady Theo. "We're going to cut his pants off now. It's best if you and Miss Sophie aren't here."

"Call us if there's a problem, John," she told him, edging Sophie towards the door. "We'll see you tomorrow and try to work out what to do with him then."

As she began climbing the stairs, Sophie realized that Lady Theo had been so caught up in looking after the boy that she hadn't commented on one glaring fact: Cousin Mary had not appeared. She must have woken up to light a candle, but why hadn't she come downstairs to help? It was almost as though she wanted to be invisible.

Sophie and Maggie sat in Billy's room the next morning while Luc, John Coachman, and the grooms searched along the Parramatta Road for his horse and signs of an attack. Although Billy seemed in a lot of pain and groaned every time he tried to turn, he still hadn't woken up by the time luncheon was served.

"It's just as well," Lady Theo said when Sophie reported this. "John suspects a couple of broken ribs. His leg was difficult to set, but it should heal straight if he stays off it. His family will have a hard time making him rest, I think."

Instead of going out in the sailboat, Sophie crept around the house and looked in on Billy every now and then. Usually Cousin Mary was in the room, sponging his face and speaking softly to him. "Maybe it will help him," she explained half-sheepishly to Sophie.

"Why didn't you come down last night?" Sophie asked.

A complicated look flashed across Cousin Mary's face — embarrassment, determination, and wariness in equal parts. "I slept through everything," she said eventually.

That was an outright lie. Sophie had seen the candlelight under her door when she'd gone upstairs to change. She knew she must have woken up to light the candle. She thought about telling Cousin Mary this, but knew that Billy's sickroom wasn't the right place.

To make matters more tense, one of their neighbours paid an afternoon call. Although Wynsham told her that Lady Theo wasn't "at home," Mrs. Sharpe insisted on seeing Lady Theo. "I've news of brigands in the area," she explained. "I know her ladyship will be grateful for the news."

"Sharpe by name, sharp by nature," Wynsham grumbled when he reported this. Mrs. Sharpe was notorious in the area. She lived in a huge house in nearby Concord, and had difficulty keeping any servants. With no one wanting to work for her, she relied on the government to assign convicts to her.

"There's too much opportunity in this country," she announced to all and sundry after she had falsely accused yet another convict of theft. "People don't know when they have it good." She was a thin, scrawny woman with a beakish kind of nose. Nobody had ever seen her supposed husband, and explanations for his absence ran from "he's run away" to "she must have murdered him with that nose of hers."

Because Mrs. Sharpe prided herself on knowing all the latest gossip, Lady Theo groaned as she set off to have tea with her unwelcome guest. "Mary, you can help me entertain her. It's the least you can do."

Cousin Mary looked mutinous. "I can't stand the woman. She wants to know every secret. I feel like making things up just so she'll go away."

"Maybe that's what you should do today. Fill her mind with an outrageous story, so that she doesn't find out about Billy."

Her smile to Cousin Mary seemed false, or so Sophie thought. Maybe Lady Theo was punishing her for sleeping through the bustle of Billy's arrival, although that didn't seem realistic. Lady Theo wasn't like that.

As though she could sense her thoughts, Lady Theo looked hard at Sophie before she spoke. "Sophie, make sure you keep an eagle eye out for Luc. He should be returning any time. Make him stay in the kitchen. Tell him to be quiet and do not let him near Mrs. Sharpe."

Mrs. Sharpe stayed longer than the polite half hour. Wynsham refreshed the silver teapot. Twice. "I even asked if she'd like her carriage brought round," he told Sophie. "She didn't take the hint. I'm sure she suspects something. Fortunately, she doesn't know what, and can't ask the right questions."

Finally, Mrs. Sharpe ran out of excuses to stay, and after saying goodbye, Lady Theo and Cousin Mary walked into the kitchen to find Sophie. "That woman is sheer torture. If I wanted to punish the convicts, I'd make them sit through a session with her," groaned

Cousin Mary. "My face feels like it's cracking because I had to keep a smile on it for so long. I need rest after that torture."

Lady Theo ignored her. "Is Luc back, Sophie?"

"Just. He's upstairs changing his clothes. The ones he had on were filthy. And Billy's awake. Well, sort of. He wakes up, then goes right back to sleep."

While they waited for Billy to wake up again, Sophie thought she had never seen anyone more battered. She suspected that he might be good-looking, but his bruises made it hard to tell. His slightly overlong blond hair curled at the ends, and he looked angelic in one of Luc's nightgowns. Sophie thought that, judging by the crinkles near his eyes, he probably laughed a lot, and she wanted him to wake so she could find out if he was as nice as he looked.

Almost as though she'd spoken out loud, Billy stirred and opened his blue eyes. He looked puzzled and seemed to be trying to work out who she and Lady Theo were. "Where am I?" he asked eventually.

"In my house in Abbotsford, near the Longbottom stockade," Lady Theo answered in a gentle voice. "I'm Lady Theodosia Thornleigh and this is my ward, Miss Sophie Mallory."

Billy tried to lower his head in a small bow, but groaned at the movement. "I'm pleased to make your acquaintance, Lady Thornleigh and Miss Mallory. I'm William Kendricks. Most people call me Billy, though."

He was a gentleman's son, Sophie decided. He spoke with a muted aristocratic accent, and, more importantly, knew what to call Lady Theo. His eyes almost closed again, but he jerked them open and stared at Lady Theo. "Do you know what happened to me? I seem to remember riding at least three miles further west than the stockade."

"Don't you remember anything?" Lady Theo asked.

"I was riding hard along the road. Suddenly, I was on the ground. Two men came out of the trees, I think, and started beating me with sticks and branches."

"Would you recognize them?"

Billy shook his head. "They had handkerchiefs over their faces. Besides, it was dark. But, I'm sure I was at least halfway between the Bath Arms and Parramatta. Where was I found?"

"In the river. You were floating near the rocks around Kissing Point. They must have thought you were dead and dumped your body." Lady Theo answered. "Tell me, why on earth were you riding at night? You must know there are robbers."

"But I wasn't," Billy asserted, trying to sit up and wincing at the pain. "Riding at night, that is. There was about an hour or so before sunset. I was trying to get to Parramatta, sleep overnight at my school, and leave at daybreak for home."

"He's right," Luc said, entering the room. "We found marks of a fight about three miles down the road. Someone said he'd seen two masked men riding off with

114

a third horse just before sunset last night. Though how he ended up in the river where he did, no one knows."

"Billy, meet my other ward, Luc Moriset. Luc, William Kendricks."

Sophie watched the two of them size each other up. They were roughly the same height and age, she thought. Then, through some kind of unspoken male communication that she didn't understand, they made up their minds and smiled. "That's my night shirt you've got on," Luc told him as he settled into a chair near the bed.

Billy smiled again, then turned to Lady Theo. "Lady Thornleigh, was everything I had with me stolen?"

She raised an eyebrow at his careful choice of words. "How would I know what you had? If there was anything in your pockets, I'm afraid it's gone, together with your horse. However, my coachman found a package tied to your chest. It saved your life by protecting you from a more savage beating."

Billy's eyes didn't leave her face as he tried to push himself up by his elbows. "Did you open it?"

Lady Theo took her time before answering. "Yes, Billy, I opened it. I was hoping to find out who you were, and how I could let your family know what had happened to you."

Billy collapsed back against the pillows. His eyes closed again, and Sophie thought he might drift back to sleep. He made an effort to force his eyes open again, and tried to sit up.

"Lady Thornleigh," he began, only to find himself gently pushed back onto the pillows by Lady Theo's hand. "Lady Thornleigh, I must take that package to my mother. Would you lend me your carriage or rent one for me? I have to leave here as soon as possible."

"The simple answer, Billy, is no. No, I won't allow you to use one of my carriages and no, I won't allow anyone to hire one. You are to remain here in bed for at least a week to give your bones a chance to heal."

"But Lady Thornleigh, you don't understand. I have to get that package to Wahmurra. I would have been there by now if I hadn't been robbed." He clenched his fists in frustration and tears drenched his eyes. "Please, Lady Thornleigh," he pleaded.

"Where's Wahmurra?" Luc asked suddenly. "Is it near here?"

"It's more than a hundred miles north of here on the north shore of Port Adams," Billy told him.

"I've got an idea," Luc said as he walked to the door. "Hold on. I'm going to get a map from John Coachman."

Billy closed his eyes as soon as Luc left the room, and even Sophie could see the lines of exhaustion on his face. She understood why Lady Theo wouldn't let him leave the bed. He looked so weak that a caterpillar could push him over.

Luc must have run all the way to the stables, because he came back a couple of minutes later, panting, and with a small map in his hand. "Here's Port Adams," he told Lady Theo, pointing to a large harbour about one hundred miles north of Sydney. There's the Hawkesbury River, about halfway between here and there. There must be a bridge somewhere."

"Ferry," Billy said weakly. "You cross the Hawkesbury by Wiseman's ferry."

"Then the answer's simple. I can be you," Luc announced. "I can probably ride as far as the Hawkesbury, if I leave now. Then, if I follow this road, I can be there by dinnertime tomorrow."

"Luc Moriset! Don't you ever learn anything?" Lady Theo exploded, for once visibly angry. "That kind of foolhardiness put Billy here into a bed for at least a week. It's cost him his horse and whatever he might have had in his pockets. So, the answer is no."

"Then please let me go," Billy pleaded.

"No to you as well. You two have more courage than sense," she told them brusquely. "However, I didn't say we wouldn't help. Luc, go upstairs and pack a change of clothes. Sophie, ring the bell and ask Wynsham to send John Coachman here. Luc can go, but only if John rounds up an armed escort."

A look of peace transformed Billy's battered face, and in spite of his bruises, Sophie thought she had never seen a more handsome boy. "Thanks, Lady Thornleigh," he said, his voice a mere thread of sound. "It really is a matter of life or death."

CHAPTER 12

For the next few days, Sophie moped around the house. Luc was off on another adventure, and she was left at home. When challenged by Lady Theo, she tried to explain herself. "He gets to do exciting things," she declared. "It's not fair. I want to have adventures, too."

"You should be careful what you wish for," Lady Theo told her. "I let him go to Wahmurra for a couple of reasons: he's used to dashing off to deliver messages, and I felt I owed him for all that he's done for us. Remember how hard he worked to find your papa when no one knew where Benjamin was?" Sophie nodded reluctantly as Lady Theo arranged sprigs of Christmas Bush, with their delicate red and yellow flowers, in vases. "As well, Billy somehow trusts Luc. I thought he'd heal better if his mind was at rest. He knows Luc will get that mysterious package to Wahmurra."

"Um," Sophie said ungraciously as she bent to pick stray pieces of bush from the floor.

Cousin Mary usually arranged the flowers. It seemed she had a knack for making certain things, besides herself, beautiful. After noticing that none of the linen was monogrammed, she had taken it upon herself to embroider Lady Theo's crest on every handkerchief, sheet, napkin, and towel she could find. "It's my contribution to the household," she had informed Lady Theo with a smile.

As Sophie handed some shoots of flowering gum to Lady Theo, she frowned as something else occurred to her. "What's in that package, anyway? Why is it a matter of life and death?"

"Medicines of some sort, I believe."

"You believe?"

Lady Theo looked wary. "There were containers I've never seen before purporting to come from a pharmacy on South Head Road. Somewhere near our other house. But there isn't a pharmacy there. There's nothing but bush."

Bush, Sophie had learned, was the multi-purpose name used in New South Wales to describe everything from forests to flowering shrubs. She tried to remember South Head Road. There were a few houses along it, but like Lady Theo, she hadn't seen an apothecary's shop. She was tempted to ask Billy what it meant when she next sat with him, but felt it would be prying. Whatever that mysterious package contained, it had been important enough for him to risk his life.

"Ah, Cousin Mary," Lady Theo's voice interrupted her thoughts. "I promised Billy that someone would read to him. Here's the book. We're up to chapter five."

Sophie saw a look of panic cross Cousin Mary's face before she controlled herself. "Maybe Sophie can do it. I'm much better at flowers than I am with books, Cousin Theo," she answered. "Why don't I finish these and put fresh ones in the bedrooms? I'll take my embroidery in with me later and talk with him then."

Lady Theo handed *Ivanhoe* to Sophie. "Go in and read, child. While Cousin Mary finishes the flowers, I'll tackle the accounts."

A couple of days later, she and Lady Theo began to fret. By their calculations, Luc should have returned. Sophie alternated between going to the Longbottom gate where she could watch the traffic on the Parramatta Road, reading to Billy, and working off her worries about Luc on the water. That particular afternoon she had paddled the canoe to her furthest limit. As she sat watching a fight among some ibises in the trees, a beautiful sloop sailed into view, moving effortlessly towards their riverside wharf.

Holding her paddle, she let the canoe drift as she watched its progress, wondering who might be calling on them. Judging from the sheer size of the boat, it might even be Governor Gipps himself. Seconds later, to her great surprise, she heard Luc's voice. "Sophie! Ahoy there!"

She waved her hand and immediately turned the canoe around. As she paddled frantically back to the dock on the bay, she wondered what on earth Luc would be doing on such a boat. By the time she beached the canoe and reached the front door of the house, the sloop was in the process of docking. Its size made the *Sophronia* look like a dinghy. It seemed like a ship from a dream. Every brass handle gleamed, its crew wore impeccably white uniforms, and a flag with an insignia Sophie couldn't identify fluttered in the breeze. Not bothering to take her dirty pinafore off, she ran down the path to the wharf where Luc was helping an elegant lady down the gangplank — a lady almost as elegant as Lady Theo. Behind her was a man who looked like Billy might in thirty years, and behind them was a girl who looked about Sophie's own age. Sophie skidded to a stop when she saw her face. It was one she had hoped she'd never see again, and once again, she was going to be made to look stupid because of her clothes.

The girl from the Governor's Garden Party looked immaculate, and she stopped at the top of the gangplank when she saw Sophie. Sophie could well imagine why. She knew she looked a mess: her hair was windblown and her pinafore had mud from the riverbank splattered all over it. She felt herself swell like a puff-fish in indignation, and for a brief moment she thought of running back to the house and hiding, or going back to the canoe and paddling far, far away. Instead, she summoned her courage, pasted a welcoming smile on her face, and walked forward.

Luc ran towards her, a wide grin on his face. "Soph! You'll never guess. I had the greatest adventure."

Sophie ignored him. "Mr. and Mrs. Kendricks? I'm Sophie Mallory. Welcome. Please excuse Luc's lack of manners."

Luc flushed. He took Sophie's hand and bowed. "Forgive me, one and all. Sophie, may I present Lord and Lady Kendricks and Miss Polly Kendricks. Of Wahmurra and Double Bay. Lord and Lady Peter, Miss Sophie Mallory."

Sophie curtsied. "My lord, my lady. Miss Kendricks. Please follow me. Billy will be so pleased to see you."

"Well done," Lady Theo told Sophie after she had shown her visitors to Billy's room. "Wynsham could not have handled the introductions any better. You greeted our guests beautifully. I'm proud of you."

"You mean proud of me after I recovered from running like a hoyden down to the dock," Sophie retorted. "I know you've taught me better, Lady Theo. But I never dreamed of Billy being so grand. He's easily the nicest lord's son I've ever met. And that's despite the fact of who his sister is."

"We'll have none of that while they're our guests, Sophie. I don't know what made you take such a dislike to the poor girl, but I don't want it obvious. Now, run along. I fancy you'll want to look respectable when we have tea."

Sophie took a couple of steps towards the stairs and stopped. "You know, I've been racking my mind, trying to remember where I'd heard the Kendricks name before. They must have that white villa across the bay from our Double Bay house. I'm sure I remember the agent saying a lord lived there."

"Yes, he did. These are our neighbours, the ones I missed meeting at Governor Gipps's Garden Party. Hurry upstairs and change, Sophie. Tea will be served in twenty minutes. Now, where's Luc?"

Wynsham led the Kendricks family into the parlour twenty minutes later. To her chagrin, Sophie noticed that Polly sat as far from her as she could get. As Lady Theo and Lord Peter did the British aristocratic ritual of connecting their families, Luc arrived in his best clothes. "I'll wager my share of the house that Lady T will find out that they're cousins," he muttered. "I swear, she's related to half of England."

While Lord Peter and Lady Theo discovered that they were indeed cousins, four times removed, his wife thanked Sophie for the hours she had spent looking after Billy. "He's in fine shape, considering his injuries. You've done everything right, keeping him occupied and allowing him to heal that much faster. We're much indebted to you."

As Sophie blushed, Lord Peter added his thanks. "Lady Theo," he went on, "how did Billy end up here? We know he was attacked miles away. Why did his good Samaritans choose your house to bring him to?" A dead silence followed his words as Sophie, Luc, and Lady Theo seemed lost in thought. "We know it must have been God's hand," he went on. "We could not have asked for anything better than the care you've all given, but it does strike me that there are several places between here and there where he might have been taken."

Sophie wondered how Lady Theo would reply. Luc seemed enamoured by Polly Kendricks's face. Lady Theo looked as uncomfortable as Sophie felt. Just as the silence was becoming too obvious, she seemed to make up her mind about Lord Peter. "I'm sure you know that the Longbottom stockade is across the bay. It's where the political convicts from Lower Canada are imprisoned. Sophie and I made their acquaintance when they captured us in Edward Ellice's house in Beauharnois, outside Montreal, during their rebellion. We attended some of their trials and came to know a few of them when we delivered goods and wrote letters for them when they were in the Montreal jail."

Polly Kendricks, Sophie noted, seemed fascinated by the story. But before she could speak, Lady Peter exclaimed, "You were captured by rebels? How terrifying!"

Sophie thought back to November 1838. It had been terrifying at times but now, in retrospect, she remembered it as a grand adventure. The real terror had come when they had found out that the British had captured her papa and that no one knew where he was. All three of them — Lady Theo, Luc, and herself — had done everything to find him. Even after they had succeeded, the terror hadn't ended because Benjamin had severe head injuries and amnesia. To this day, Sophie wasn't quite sure what her father remembered, mainly because he had used his amnesia to shield his sons, her brothers, from their participation in the rebellion. By rights, it should have been Albert, Bartholomew, and Clarence Mallory who were in Longbottom, not her innocent Papa.

"Actually," Luc interrupted with a rather belligerent tone to his voice, "my brother Marc is one of them." He held his head high and continued. "He was a leader in the rebellion, but he didn't do what they convicted him of. His trial was a sham."

Lord and Lady Peter seemed to take these revelations in stride. "So, I'm assuming in my role of Billy's father, and not that of a magistrate, that some rebels were illegally outside the stockade when Billy was attacked."

"Not *when* he was attacked," Luc retorted, looking hurt that anyone should think so badly of his brother and his comrades. "They found him in the river near Kissing Point a couple of hours later. Well after dark. What's more, if they hadn't been out of the stockade, he would have drowned. Legal or not, they saved his life."

"I'm aware of that, Luc. I suspected something like that might be the answer. You have my word that I won't make trouble." He ran his fingers through his hair in exactly the same way that Sophie had seen Billy do. "The longer I live, the less life surprises me. William Wentworth, who lives farther down the South Head Road from us in Vaucluse, talked to me about applying for some of these men when the time comes for their assignment. It seems that they have a great reputation for their craftsmanship and honesty. Wentworth says they're going to be prized workers."

"How does one go about getting a convict assigned? Is there a process?" Lady Theo asked, her voice showing little of the interest Sophie knew she must feel.

Lord Peter's eyes twinkled. "I can introduce you to Major Barney. And, if you had anyone particular in mind, I'm sure he'll try to accommodate you."

"Am I too young to have someone assigned to me, Lord Peter?" Luc asked.

"Someone, like your brother? You're too insubstantial, I'm afraid, young Luc. You need to own property."

"But ...," Luc began, before seeing something on Lady Theo's face that made him keep quiet.

Lady Peter quickly smoothed the situation. "Lady Thornleigh, we are all quite desperately grateful to you. I agree that Billy can be carried downstairs tomorrow. He'll be less restless if he can sit outside and enjoy the warm air. I know he can be a horrible patient. I wonder too, seeing that Peter has an Executive Council meeting tomorrow afternoon, if Polly and I could come here? She, I know, will be delighted to spend time with Billy and your two, and I thought that you might like to sail around the harbour for an hour or two. It's very soothing."

When Lady Theo smiled and agreed, Sophie fiddled with the porcelain dog on the table beside her and felt like screaming. Lady Theo would be happy, Billy would be happy, Polly would be happy, and Luc, judging from the fatuous look on his face, would be in alt, the highest of heavens. Sophie, however, would not. She'd be in the doldrums. What terrible misfortune had brought Polly Kendricks into her world? It wasn't fair.

CHAPTER 13

By luncheon the next day, Sophie was thoroughly disgruntled. Luc had been at his most superior that morning, claiming the need to spend time with "his" workers to see what had been going on in his absence. The Canadians hadn't left the canoe on her side of the bay, so for once, she couldn't paddle off her frustration. Even Billy contributed to her sense that the world was against her. John Coachman had arranged for him to be fitted with new splints and crutches that Lady Peter had suggested, so he had been carried to the stables. Judging from the occasional shouts of laughter, Luc had finished his work and joined him there. Sophie hadn't been asked.

She hadn't heard much about Luc's trip to Billy's home. At dinner, Luc had described something of his mad dash north, but beyond saying that it had been an adventure he wouldn't have missed for the world, he had spoken mostly about Wahmurra and the Kendricks.

According to him, Wahmurra was a huge estate with more than 400,000 acres. It was self-sufficient with its own brickyard, dairy, timber mills, and farms. As Luc talked, Lady Theo's eyes lit up and she began questioning him. Sophie thought she knew why. Wahmurra sounded very much like the property that Lady Theo and her group of investors hoped to buy.

To make matters worse, Luc liked the Kendricks family. His voice reflected his admiration whenever he spoke of it. There were two sets of twins — Billy and Polly — and a younger pair — James and John. "It's no wonder that Polly's such a great girl," he enthused. "Her brothers have made sure of it."

"My brothers didn't make sure of it for me," Sophie commented, feeling very jealous.

If she were to be honest, she still felt jealous. When Lady Peter took Lady Theo off on their river cruise, she would be by herself on the outside. Luc would probably look at Polly as though she was the most wonderful girl in the world. Billy, of course, would want to hear all about Wahmurra, and they'd all talk about things she hadn't seen and didn't know. She would much rather be out on the Kendricks' yacht, even if it meant listening while Lady Theo and Lady Peter talked.

And that reminded her of yet another puzzle: Billy's mysterious package, which no one wanted to talk about. Not even Lady Peter.

And why did everyone call her "Lady Peter"? Her name was Christina. Why wasn't she called Lady Christina?

"Because Lord Peter isn't a real lord," Lady Theo told her at lunch.

"His father is a duke and his brother is a marquis," Luc added. "He gets to be called 'lord' because of his father, and his wife gets to be called 'lady' because of him. That's why she's Lady Peter," he finished, looking very smug as he explained the intricacies of the British peerage to Sophie.

She still didn't understand. "Well, if she's called Lady Peter because she's married to Lord Peter, why isn't Lord Peter called Lord Whatever-his-father's name?"

Luc gave her a pitying look and changed the subject. "John's going to carry Billy outside after lunch. When Polly comes, we can sit by the verandah and he can see what's going on."

Sophie hadn't finished her questions. "Should we be calling them Lord Billy and Lady Polly?" she asked Lady Theo.

"No, dear," she began, only to be interrupted by Wynsham.

"Young Jimmy just ran in to tell us that you can see the sloop, my lady. It's ten minutes away."

Lady Theo stood up. "So early. Sophie, go upstairs and change. I asked Maggie to put the pink dress out."

Sophie left the room but stopped at the bottom of

the stairs. She had liked the pink dress in London; she wasn't so sure about it now. Its embroidered flowers seemed too fussy for a casual afternoon, and she really didn't want to sit around in it making polite conversation with Polly Kendricks. Sailing the harbour seemed much better, but Lady Theo would never allow her to leave their guests. Still, Sophie thought, what Lady Theo didn't know, she couldn't forbid. Even if she had to hide below deck, it would be preferable to an afternoon watching Luc make gooey eyes at Polly Kendricks. Quickly, before she could have second thoughts, she ran out the side door, through the shrubbery, to the bushes near the wharf.

She had just reached them when the Kendrickses arrived. Immaculate sailors made the boat secure, then helped a sulky-looking Polly down the gangplank. Luc appeared from the side of the house, made his bow to Lady Peter, and led Polly towards the verandah where Billy waited.

Lady Peter navigated the gangplank, but before she'd walked more than a couple of yards, Lady Theo came out of the house. She had changed her clothes and, for a moment, Sophie wondered if she had noticed the pink dress still on the bed as she'd walked by Sophie's room.

Lady Theo looked smart in a white skirt and blouse with navy trimming. A long navy ribbon on her white straw hat emphasized the nautical theme. As she neared the wharf, she stopped and Sophie wondered if she'd seen her. Then she walked over to Lady Peter and said something so softly that Sophie couldn't hear. She saw Lady Peter grimace, speak to one of the sailors, then both women turned away from the water. They walked towards the set of outdoor chairs under a flowering gum tree and sat facing the bushes where Sophie hid.

They chatted for a few moments and seemed to find much to laugh about. Sophie felt chagrined. She hadn't counted on Lady Theo asking Lady Peter to sit and talk. Now, Sophie couldn't get aboard the sloop without being seen. She wondered what they found so interesting, and eased forward a little towards the gum tree so that she could hear their conversation.

At first, she felt that she needn't have bothered. Lady Theo was talking about the difficulty of getting female servants who hadn't been convicts. Then Lady Peter said something that made Sophie's ears prick up. "I have to congratulate you, Theodosia," she went on, "for the beautiful manners of your wards. My four are only that well behaved in their sleep."

"Billy's behaviour had been exemplary. Beyond reproach," Lady Theo protested.

"And Sophie? How do you manage to get her to look so beautiful?" Lady Peter continued. "I swear, Polly is quite the hoyden compared to her. Although she has a wardrobe full of beautiful dresses, I think she has only worn three since I bought them."

"One time, surely, was the Governor's Garden Party. Did she tell you about that?"

Lady Peter laughed and muttered something that Sophie couldn't hear. She seemed to pitch her voice higher as she added, "I must admit that I'm hoping Sophie's elegance will inspire her. Nothing else seems to. She's happiest when chasing off with Billy on horseback or messing around in her boat. She should have been a boy like the rest of them, poor soul."

"Well, on behalf of Sophie, thank you for your kind words. I'm afraid that I can't claim any credit. Sophie's parents are responsible for her manners. Of course, I give some guidance as to what to wear, but she has innate good taste."

"I only hope she can transfer some to Polly," Lady Peter said as she rose gracefully to her feet. "Let's get on board to see if the breezes off the river will cool us. But," she added as she stopped very near to the bushes where Sophie was hiding, "I'd give a small fortune to find out why my Polly is awed by your Sophie."

"And I'd give a lot more to find out why Sophie has taken Polly in such instant dislike. It's not like her, at all. She's friendly, always. Up to now, that is."

They know where I am, Sophie thought. *This is Lady Theo's way of telling me that she knows I was trying to run away, and that I'm to go back to the house and be friendly.* She frowned and dug a stick into the sandy soil. She poked it around then jumped back as a succession of large black ants appeared. After hurriedly making a dirt barrier between herself and the ants, she put her arms around her legs and began to think.

Everyone, she decided, had probably been right. She had made a mountain out of a molehill about the dresses. Sometimes, though, it seemed impossible not to get angry over little things. Strangely enough, Cousin Mary seemed to understand that better than Lady Theo and called it the pain of growing up.

She now realized that she'd painted herself into a corner by making Polly dislike her. That meant Billy would as well — once he figured out Sophie had offended his twin — and Sophie did not want to lose Billy's good opinion of her. After a couple of minutes of further thought, she jumped to her feet.

Eureka! When she started back towards the house, she was smiling. She had a plan.

CHAPTER 14

When Sophie reached the side verandah, she saw Billy resting on the padded bamboo chaise lounge, his broken leg supported by a pile of cushions. Polly sat upright on a chair next to him and seemed to be telling an amusing story. Luc, smiling, stood against a pillar, watching the convicts load logs onto a barge on the Longbottom side of the bay.

He saw Sophie first and took one step towards her. "Sophie!" he exclaimed, his voice showing his surprise at her dirty and dishevelled state.

She ignored him and walked over to Polly. "I've realized that I haven't checked my traps for more than a day. Would you like to come with me?"

Polly stood, staring at Sophie in apparent disbelief. "I'd love to," she began, then indicated her dress. "But Mama would have a fit if I ruined this."

"I could lend you an old dress, if you'd like."

"Sophie, what are you up to?" Luc challenged. "You can't go off and leave us here."

"Can't I? You and Billy have lots to talk about. It's a boating afternoon for all the women in our families. Right, Polly?"

Polly looked at the outrage on Billy and Luc's faces. "Right," she agreed, laughing and blowing a kiss to them.

"Come along," Sophie urged. "I've something to show you." She almost dragged Polly through the house and up to her bedroom. She walked across the room, opened her wardrobe, and beckoned. "Look!"

Polly stared at a dress that was almost identical to the one she was wearing. "It's another one that's the same. But, I don't understand. Madame Hallé swore this was the only one she'd made. I went back to her shop and asked. What a liar."

"Maybe not," Sophie told her. "When we first arrived, a Mrs. Halladay came and asked if she could make sketches of some of my clothes. She said she planned to set up an exclusive shop, and wanted to have the latest patterns. Lady Theo wasn't there, so I let her. You must have bought some that she made from those sketches. That's why we were identical at the Governor's reception. I wore my best dress that had been made in London. Yours, which was almost identical, must have been made by Mrs. Halladay. I've thought and thought about it, and it's the only thing that makes sense." She pulled a work dress out of the wardrobe and handed it to Polly. "Now, this I can guarantee is not made by Mrs. Halladay. Should I call my maid?"

"Could you help with these?" Polly asked, indicating the row of pearl buttons running from the neck of the dress to its waist at the back. "I can't reach all of them."

Sophie began the unbuttoning. "You know, Mrs. Halladay would make a fortune if she ever opened a store in London. Her sewing on this is far better than that on mine."

"She wouldn't be able to open a place like hers in London," Polly replied. "She's an ex-convict."

"She's done her time," Sophie argued, as she began buttoning up the work dress.

"But she'll always be known as a convict, or an emancipist. There's such a stigma attached to convicts. Even men who have made good, like Simeon Lord, are not always accepted in the best circles."

"What about their children?"

"Ah, that's another story entirely. At Billy's school, half the students are children of convicts. At least, according to him."

"And the other half?" Sophie questioned.

"Children of some of the wealthiest men in New South Wales. It's one of the reasons Mama likes his school so much. It's pretty hard for those boys to be snobby when they have the son of a convict sitting next to them."

Sophie shrugged. She'd have to think it over. It seemed unfair that Papa would be always stigmatized, and that she wouldn't. As Polly pulled a pinafore over the work dress, she took her hand and pulled. "Come on. Have you ever canoed?"

About two hours later, Polly and Sophie paddled back to the house, muddy, wet, and very happy. Their friendship had progressed to the point where they had a million questions to ask each other, yet the most important answers had already been given. They had a total of seven crabs in their basket and two lobsters. The Thornleigh household would eat well that night.

As they came in sight of the house, Sophie groaned when she saw the Kendricks' sloop at the wharf. "They're back. If Lady Theo sees you looking like this, I'll be in trouble."

Polly laughed. "Mama won't mind. I get far dirtier than this messing around with Billy."

"That won't matter to Lady Theo," Sophie gloomily predicted, steering towards the bay-side dock. "Let's go in the back way. If we're lucky, we can get hot water for a bath without anyone knowing."

Cook didn't care how dirty they looked once she saw the contents of the baskets. She pointed to the back staircase and ordered the pantry maid to carry hot water to Sophie's room, and when Sophie and Polly left the kitchen, she was muttering about sauces.

"Your house is like ours," Polly said as she peeled her

sodden stockings off.

"Oh, how?"

"I have friends who have never been in their kitchens. They wouldn't think of it. They say the servants wouldn't respect them if they're too familiar. You're like us. You treat them like people. I can tell that they like you."

"If you knew what poor Eloise and John Coachman have been through, you'd know we couldn't treat them any differently. In fact," she broke off and giggled, "they're our landlords."

"Your landlords? How?"

While they bathed, and Maggie helped them dress, Sophie told the story of the purchase of the house. Polly looked at Maggie, who was beaming with pleasure. "You must be proud, Maggie."

"That I am, miss. It's like Miss Sophie says: a miracle. My father and mother, my four brothers, and I left Ireland fourteen years ago to have a new life in Canada. Everyone, except me, got cholera and went to be with the blessed Jesus. The nuns in Montreal cared for me. I got a job at a good hotel there as a maid. Next thing I know, I meet Miss Sophie. She's in trouble, so I help her. Lady Theo asks me if I'd like to be Miss Sophie's maid, even if it means coming here." She finished buttoning Sophie's dress and began brushing her curls.

Polly smoothed one of her own curls back into place. "You weren't worried about coming here? Weren't you scared of the convicts?"

Maggie stared at her. "Not when I know some," she began, then quickly looked at Sophie. When Sophie gave a slight, negative nod, Maggie resumed her story. "Canada was supposed to be the new start, miss. But, it turned out to be full of sorrow for me. New South Wales sounded like an adventure, even though I had to sail almost around the world to get here. And, now, I'm a landlord. Well, partly one. Like I said earlier, it's a miracle."

Polly smiled. "I believe it is."

"Come over to this mirror, Polly," Sophie called. "Let's see what we look like."

When they saw the reflection of themselves standing side by side, they both laughed. "Let's go down," Sophie said. "I can't wait to see everyone's faces."

CHAPTER 15

Sophie and Polly stood in the doorway, in their identical dresses, a picture of solidarity. During the time they'd spent pulling fish traps out of the water and scrabbling around in mud for crabs, they'd become firm friends. They laughed as they walked into the room.

Cousin Mary had made an appearance, Sophie noted. She sat in a corner of the room, her sewing on her lap, and looked as though she'd burst into laughter at any moment. Sophie couldn't figure out what exactly amused her so much. The identical dresses weren't that funny.

From that moment, though, it seemed that they split into pairs. Billy and Luc talked incessantly, telling each other tall stories, Sophie and Polly were still in the intense getting to know each other phase of friendship, and Lady Peter and Lady Theo seemed happy to have another woman to talk to. Cousin Mary, the outsider by her own choice, watched their comings and goings with her strange smile, but disappeared to her room whenever Lord Peter visited.

As Billy still couldn't walk — not even with his new crutches — he and Luc stayed in Abbotsford. The other four divided their time between their two homes. "I've never had a friend that I could talk to as easily as I do with Polly," Sophie told Lady Theo one afternoon when John Coachman was driving them to Double Bay. "It's different from you and Luc. Even from Papa. I tell Polly silly things that I know you wouldn't be interested in. I tell her about the horrible girls at my school in England, and she tells me about some of her friends here. You know, Cousin Mary figured them out almost immediately: they do judge people by their clothes. Polly says sometimes she deliberately wears her old clothes to confuse them. I think it's silly to judge people by what they wear, don't you?"

"Of course, I do. You have to learn though, child, that clothes can also be a weapon." Lady Theo smiled at Sophie. After a sharp smell permeated the carriage, she sniffed and hurriedly closed the windows. "I don't know when I'll get used to the smell of cattle markets. I know we have to pass them when we go through Sydney, but goodness knows, I wish there was some other route we could take."

Sophie put her handkerchief over her nose. "I don't know whether it's better to choke or put up with the smell."

They sat silently while John negotiated their way through the quieter and less-smelly New South Head Road. With a sigh of relief, Lady Theo rolled down the window again. "I do know what you mean about having a friend you can talk to, Sophie. I'm so glad I met Christina. I don't feel quite so alone anymore."

"You're not alone," Sophie argued. "You have me. And Papa."

"Papa can't tell me which women to avoid, which ones gossip, which ones are malicious. Besides, as you said yourself, there are some things you can talk about with a good friend that you can't with family."

"Umm." Sophie liked the idea of having Polly as her friend, but didn't like the thought that Lady Theo might share things with Lady Peter that she wouldn't with her. She supposed Luc and Billy were busy exchanging secrets as well.

One afternoon after they returned to Abbotsford ahead of the Kendricks, Sophie dragged Luc out in the *Sophronia* to catch the evening's dinner. At first it felt strange to be sitting close to the water. As she leaned over the side to pull a couple of crabs from a trap, she realized how easily she'd become used to the Kendricks' sloop. After she'd put the crabs in her bucket she asked, "What do you make of Cousin Mary?"

Luc concentrated on navigating his way past an oversized buoy. "Well," he said, throwing his head back and letting the wind tousle his hair, "I admit that I was wrong about her. In the beginning. I thought she'd be out gal-livanting around the place, getting herself and Lady Theo into all sorts of trouble. I still think there's a chance that might happen, but it's not because she's a flirt, which I thought at first. If anything, she's the opposite."

"Ah," Sophie said. "You've noticed that too."

"Noticed what?"

"That she disappears when strangers come to the house. It's as though she's scared of meeting them. You know the night Billy came? Well, she woke up like the rest of us, but didn't come down. I know she did, because I saw that she'd lit a candle."

Luc counted their haul of crabs and fish. "I think that will do us. I know Cook is roasting beef and ham as well." He pushed the tiller so that the boat turned into the wind and home. "I don't think Mary's met Lord Peter yet, has she? Want to bet that she'll be too sick to eat dinner with us?"

Sophie looked at him indignantly. "I'm not going to bet with you. You still owe me ten shillings because I learned to sail faster than you did."

"Come on, Soph. Double or nothing."

"Absolutely not. I might as well just give you the ten shillings because I, too, think she'll find some excuse to eat her dinner in her room."

Luc made a face. "Well, why let's bet on whether or not Lady T notices? I can't believe she's letting Cousin Mary get away with everything. When it comes to us, she's as sharp as a tack. She seems to know what I'm going to do before I do it."

"You're not that hard to figure out," Sophie told him. She pushed a crab that was trying to get out of the bucket back into it, then searched for a lid. When she spoke again, her voice was softer, "It's funny, Luc. Even though we're maybe imagining things like she can't read, or that she'll probably manage to avoid eating with us, I still like her. When she's actually doing things with us, she's nice."

"You're just saying that because she puts flowers in your bedroom," Luc retorted.

"No, it's not just that. I saw companions, like she was supposed to be, in England. Usually, they were like ghosts. Some fluttered around, but didn't do anything substantial. The others were sometimes downright nasty. I felt that they resented the fact that they were like servants who didn't get paid, and they made sure everyone noticed them. Sometimes they'd be too sweet, I felt I'd gag. Other times, they told on people, saying all the time, that they didn't mean to get anyone into trouble, when all the time, everyone knew that they jolly well did. They were truly horrible. The bottom line, though, was they all wore drab, don't-notice-me kind of clothes. Cousin Mary is different."

"Well, I like her too, even though she surprised me. Do you think that's why Lady T doesn't notice things?"

Sophie grabbed the rope and got ready to jump out to tie the *Sophronia* up. "I don't know," she said, her voice troubled. "Maybe, she's got a blind spot where Cousin Mary's concerned. Anyway, let's hurry. The Kendricks should be here at any moment."

Cook outdid herself with dinner, and seven happy people later sat on the verandah in comfortable bamboo chairs to watch the sunset. As Luc and Sophie predicted, Cousin Mary had taken ill suddenly and kept to her room. Lady Theo had raised an eyebrow when that message was conveyed, but whether or not she'd begun to see the pattern in her cousin's illnesses, Sophie couldn't tell. She sat quietly, listening to Lord Peter tell stories about Wahmurra's beginning, when she heard rustling sounds in the bushes leading up from the bay-side dock.

Lord Peter did as well. He stopped talking, half got out of his chair, then sat down again. "There's someone or something in your bushes, Theo," he said. "Shall I see what it is?"

Lady Theo looked towards the bushes, then back towards him. "I don't think there's any problem," she said loudly.

Almost immediately, Marc and Benjamin appeared in their convict clothes. Marc carried a posy of flowers tied up with a red ribbon. He presented them to Lady Theo with a bow, "Pretty flowers for a pretty lady."

"Oh, Marc. Thank you," Lady Theo said, slightly flustered. "I have some guests I'd like you to meet."

Luc immediately went to stand next to his brother. At the same time, Sophie walked, half-ran to her father and grabbed one of his hands. While Lady Theo made the introductions, Sophie studied the Kendricks family. Billy looked singularly unsurprised, and she suspected he must have seen some of the comings and goings from the Longbottom side of the bay. Lady Peter smiled, and her "Pleased to make your acquaintance" seemed genuine. Lord Peter acknowledged the introductions stiffly, and Sophie guessed that the magistrate part of him warred with the father of Billy, who had been rescued with the help of Marc and Papa. Polly's reaction was different. She looked hurt, and Sophie guessed that she thought Sophie might have told her this secret in one of their endless conversations.

For a while, the earlier lazy atmosphere seemed a mirage. Lady Peter tried to make comfortable conversation, helped by Billy, as best he could. Papa wore his negotiating face, as though he was working to make Marc and himself acceptable to Lord Peter. "I suppose you would like an explanation," he said.

"Not really," Lord Peter told him. "I understand about your comings and goings. I am reminded of them every time I look at Billy. I suppose I am surprised, though. You look far too intelligent to have played the fool as you did at your trial."

Everyone looked amazed. Lady Theo turned to him. "Peter, his sons owe their lives to the fact that Benjamin took the blame for them."

"So I understand. I don't know if I would have done

the same, Mr. Mallory. I would never expect betrayal from Billy. Your sons' behaviour must have been a bitter pill."

Sophie thought Papa looked at Lord Peter as if he was trying to work him out. Lady Theo looked dumbfounded because, Sophie guessed, she hadn't told any of the Kendricks about the trial. But it was Sophie's turn to be surprised by Lord Peter.

"And you, young lady, made an excellent witness. I think maybe your love for your father, shown at his trial, must have helped him balance your brothers' actions."

"How do you know all this?" Sophie asked.

"Ah. Sydney might be almost as far away from Canada as you can get, but sensational news has a way of bridging distance. Someone took notes during all the trials and published them in a book. When I found the connection between us and your Longbottom men, I managed to buy it. Your trial was in volume one, Mr. Moriset; yours in volume two, Mr. Mallory."

Luc looked at him, his eyes alight with excitement. "Then you know Marc's trial was a sham. He should have been let off."

Lord Peter smiled. "I agree that his trial was almost a farce. But, as a magistrate sworn to uphold the laws of Queen Victoria ..."

"Lady Theo's Cousin Victoria," Luc muttered.

Lord Peter ignored him. "I wanted to say, Mr. Moriset, that although your trial was irregular, I thought you were exceedingly lucky that it was. I gained the impression you were one of the leaders of that rebellion, and that the other leaders in your area were hanged. I think you owe your life to my counterpart who lied through his teeth at your court martial. You should be very grateful to him."

"Bah," started Luc, but Marc clamped a hand on his shoulder.

"Quiet," he ordered. "Sir, in my sane moments, I realize that. I suppose some part of Benjamin's acceptance of his imprisonment has rubbed off on me. If I stood before God and was asked if I considered Sydney a fair punishment, I would answer 'yes.' As you pointed out, I did lead my men. I took over when Mr. Cardinal was captured, and others who did far less were hanged. I know that, and in my deepest heart, I am grateful that Mr. McDonald's hatred of me made him lie."

Wynsham broke the tension by appearing with a tray of refreshing drinks. Both Marc and Papa took one, and as they stood drinking together, Lord Peter walked over to them. To Sophie's relief, and she supposed the relief of everyone else, he shook both their hands. As he remained talking to them, she saw the broad smile Billy and Luc exchanged, and the pleased smiles on Lady Theo and Lady Peter's faces. Polly, however, hid her face. Obviously, she was still not pleased with Sophie.

Sighing, she walked over to Polly and sat in the chair next to her. "I'm sorry I didn't tell you. It was a secret. Don't you have secrets you can't tell anyone?"

149

Polly looked up suddenly and, as she turned to her mother, Billy laughed. "Don't we just."

Both Sophie and Luc looked over to Billy. The teasing light died out of his eyes as he seemed to realize what he'd blurted out. Polly's eyes looked stormy.

Lady Peter spoke quietly as her husband returned to her side. "Every family has things it doesn't discuss easily. That's why they're secret."

"To change the topic," Lord Peter interrupted, smiling at his daughter, "Theo, I have an invitation for you. And, of course, Sophie. Luc, I've talked this over with your brother. He and Mr. Mallory both think it's a good idea. Please invite us to dinner again for two days from now. This time we will come on our boat and stay on it overnight. Then, in the morning, would the three of you sail home with us to Wahmurra? Going by water is the easiest, safest way. What do you say, Theo?"

Lady Theo looked over to Papa, and Sophie saw him give a small nod. "We'd be delighted. There's no need for your boat to come here. John Coachman can easily deliver us to your house in Double Bay."

Lord Peter smiled. "What? And deprive me of a night's drinking at the Bath Arms with a couple of convicts?"

Luc seemed elated by the prospect. He jumped up and ran across to his brother. "Can I come?" he asked.

"Not on your life," Marc asked. "I'll be asking Lord Peter about Billy's school. You know you hate talking about schools."

Luc sat down and looked, in Sophie's opinion, almost like a deflated soufflé. Just as she thought about teasing Luc, Papa caught her eye. "Don't feel left out, Sophie. I'm interested in finding out about Polly's school as well." As Luc hooted with laughter, Sophie tried to recover her composure. "I *was* going to ask about Cousin Mary."

"I'd like her to stay here," Lady Theo answered, unaware of the startled look Sophie gave. "She's a distant cousin and not quite used to things in this new country. She's ill tonight. Otherwise, you would have met her, Peter."

Sophie saw Luc say something to Billy, something which made him grin. He looked excited by the thought of going home, even though, Sophie supposed, he'd have to be carried everywhere. She, herself, was wildly excited as well. Finally, after all these months, she'd have something resembling an adventure.

CHAPTER 16

Wahmurra was on the north shore of Port Adams, and Sophie fell in love with it at first sight. It seemed a magical place with the afternoon sun turning the walls of the house into glorious gold.

Built on a low hill above the wharf, it seemed a majestic version of the typical New South Wales house — two storeys, with a wide verandah running around the lower floor. Vines, in glorious purple flower, climbed their way around the columns supporting the second one. The rooms on the ground floor had French doors opening onto the verandah.

"Who looks after the gardens?" Lady Theo asked as they climbed the stairs to the house.

"I do," Lady Peter answered. "With the help of a head gardener from England and a native from one of the islands in the Pacific. Charles looks after the more traditional flowers — we've planted daffodils and hyacinths to bloom in winter and there are wisteria trellises in one of the more formal gardens. Samu's responsible for the bougainvillea, the flame and jacaranda trees. We also have Chien-Ming, who guards his kitchen gardens as jealously as the others do theirs."

Maybe that was what made the place look so magical, Sophie thought. It was the mixture of things. She had to admit she'd never seen such a variety of plant life before. As they approached the house, a good-looking man in his thirties came out of the house and walked towards them.

"This is Mr. White, our overseer," Lady Peter said, and she began the introductions. When she finished, she looked at him searchingly, "How are you, Thomas? Recovered yet?"

"Almost. Thanks to you and your medicines. Otherwise, I'm sure I'd be dead," Mr. White answered. "Shall I organize a chair for young Billy to be carried in?"

"It's been arranged."

Later, just before bedtime, Sophie sat outside her room, looking out at Port Adams as darkness slowly enveloped it. It really was huge, and she easily believed Lord Peter, who had said that it, rather than Port Jackson, Sydney's harbour, would have been chosen if it had been discovered first. "The whole British fleet could fit in easily," he'd explained.

It was more circular than Port Jackson, and dotted with islands. Sophie tried to count them but gave up after thirteen. Directly below her, a great ocean-going merchant schooner swung lazily at anchor. Lord Peter said that Wahmurra imported many supplies directly from England. In turn, it exported timber. Sophie knew that her Papa would be interested, because the timber trade was to be their mainstay once he was released from assignment.

In the morning, there was a soft knock on her door and Luc whispered, "Soph? Come on. Let's explore before breakfast."

Sophie didn't know about that. "Shouldn't we wait for Polly or someone to show us around?"

"They won't be up for ages. "Come on. We can look around by ourselves." Sophie still felt doubtful until Luc said the magic words. "Soph, it will be an adventure. One, just for ourselves."

If Wahmurra had been magical the night before, it was equally so in the crisp air of dawn. Bits of fog fluttered around like the bolls of cotton Sophie had once seen at her London school. To her delight, clusters of kangaroos grazed on the dewy grass, but no matter how quiet she tried to be, she couldn't get close enough to touch one. A sleepy possum scrambled over a log, and fish jumped in the harbour. Birds welcomed the new day raucously — kookaburras laughed, galahs squawked, and currawongs trilled their haunting cry.

Sophie skipped for sheer happiness as she followed Luc along the main road out of the complex and past a large building that Lady Peter had called the Barracks.

Somewhere behind it, she could hear a cornet play "*Reveille*," and she imagined soldiers springing out of bed, ready for a day of doing whatever they did on the Wahmurra estate. The road led down the hill to a small creek, which Luc insisted they jump over.

"I'll fall in," Sophie tried to object.

"So what? Who's going to care? It's wonderful, here. Like being at home."

Maybe that was Wahmurra's magic. It made Sophie feel at home, like nothing else had done since she'd left Malloryville. If somehow Papa could have come, it would have been perfect. Wahmurra had everything. Wonderful scenery, a wonderful family, and it was far away from everything.

"Our Canadians would have a wonderful time here," Luc said suddenly. "Look at the oyster beds. They'd make a fortune from those shells."

"How? Why would people buy oyster shells without the oysters?"

"I didn't know, either. Marc had to explain it to me. Lime's very rare here."

"Lime? The fruit?"

Luc laughed. "No, silly. Lime is something used to make mortar, the stuff between bricks. The shells get crushed, then mixed with sand and water, and, voilà, limestone when it hardens. Come on, forget brick-making. I'll race you to the church over there. Ten shillings says I get there first."

Sophie was glad he took off before she agreed, because he had a good twenty-yard lead on her. Nevertheless, she held her skirts high and ran as fast as she could. Flushed and panting, she almost collided with a man as she reached the church and he came out the door.

"Goodness, me," he exclaimed, holding her up so she wouldn't fall. "I rarely have anyone so eager to come for morning prayers."

Sophie looked at Luc, who shrugged. "I ... Thank you." She stammered.

The man was huge and looked to be very strong. "The folks at the big house usually wait for their chaplain's service after breakfast. I'm Dan Cole, but everyone calls me Preacher Dan. Welcome to our church."

While they were talking, Sophie noticed people, mainly men, sidle by them into the church. Most seemed to be farm labourers, already dressed in their working clothes. She looked at Luc, a question in her eyes. He gave a quick nod, so she accepted Preacher Dan's arm and allowed him to lead her to the front pew.

Preacher Dan's service was quick, and his sermon mercifully short. He spoke of showing love to everyone, no matter how vile they seemed. "He mustn't have been a convict," Luc commented as they walked down the church aisle.

"He was and is," one of the men told him. "Transported for life, the preacher was. No, he knows what he's talking about. He was here in the days of old Bundy. Poor Dan got his regular share of whippings."

"I can't imagine anyone being able to whip him," Luc said.

"Well, in those days, the soldiers used to oversee the punishments. Bundy was the overseer then and he'd tell them how many lashes, and they'd make sure we got 'em. Once Lady Peter came, everything changed."

"Oh. How?"

A shuttered look crossed the man's face, as though someone had told him not to talk anymore. He muttered about the cows having to be milked, and almost fled from the church. Sophie turned to Luc, to see if he had an explanation, but he only shrugged. She couldn't imagine Polly's father agreeing to such horrible punishments, and she realized that was one more question to ask Polly, once Polly got over her snit.

By the time they'd reached the church's front door, most people had left. After shaking Preacher Dan's hand, Luc asked, "Are you the minister here?"

"Every morning and Sunday," Dan answered. The rest of the time, you'll find me in the smithy. I'm Wahmurra's blacksmith."

Well, Sophie thought, that explained the muscles. Blacksmiths were very strong. They had to handle horses who mightn't want their hooves shod and make all kinds of farm implements. And keeping their furnaces alight was an extremely hard job in itself. "Let's go," she said to Luc, after promising to visit the smithy and shaking Dan's calloused hand.

"It's still too early for breakfast," he answered. "Let's find our way through the bush via the back way."

"What about snakes?" Sophie asked, remembering Wynsham's many warnings.

"Pooh. We won't see any. Besides, you've got your boots on, haven't you?"

Sophie still hadn't made her mind up when Luc started walking up the hill behind the church, almost at a right angle to the main house. "I bet you're too scared," he called out.

"One of these days you'll have to pay me," Sophie shouted as she started after him.

Once they reached the bush, she found new delights every few yards along the way. Banksia, with a ray of sunlight illuminating a dewdrop; the dappled pattern of bark on a gum tree; a stand of redwoods that reminded her of the trees in Vermont. As they kept climbing, even Luc became awed by the natural beauty around him. "Lord Peter says that some of the trees here are among the highest in the entire world. He says they cut down one that was almost three hundred feet high."

Sophie tried to imagine a tree that tall, but couldn't. She also couldn't tell which direction they should be going. "Luc! Are you sure this is the right way?"

"Positive. Listen, I can hear the creek."

The creek was no longer the quiet stream which

meandered its way into Port Adams near the church. Instead, it splashed over tumbled rocks and old branches of trees. "How will we get across?" she asked.

"We'll have to jump it," Luc answered, sizing it up carefully. "The ground around here looks hard. If we take a run at it, Bob's your uncle. No worries."

Sophie looked where Luc stood. His heel had already sunk a good quarter inch into the mud of the creek bank. "I think we should go back. I don't think I can jump it."

"I know, little girl," Luc mocked. "Ten shillings says you won't even try. Watch me. Then, try." With that, he walked back several feet. He stood still for a moment, rocked, then ran towards the creek, exploding into a jump once he reached its edge. The ground where he'd taken off was too soft. As one foot sank into it, it threw him off balance, and he landed on the mess of stones in the middle of the creek.

"Don't worry, it will save you having a bath," Sophie laughed. "I'll find a branch and pull you out."

"Hurry, Soph. I think I've broken my ankle."

Sophie stopped in mid-laugh. A look of intense pain enveloped Luc's face. He tried to smile, but it was more like a grimace than anything. "I won't be long," she reassured him. "There has to be a strong stick somewhere."

There wasn't anything long enough near the creek, so she turned into the bush. Scrabbling around for sticks, she didn't hear movement behind her, so that when she straightened and found herself looking straight into the black face of an aboriginal man, she was too frightened to do anything other than stand still. The man muttered something, but, of course, she couldn't understand him. A roughly made bag hung around his neck, and he carried the kind of stick she was looking for. He gestured towards her, and she thought she'd turn to stone.

She'd been brought up on stories of settlers being scalped and the Hurons pulling Jean de Brebeuf's heart out of his chest. Her most recent memory of native peoples was the rather pathetic aboriginals she'd seen in Sydney. Dressed in cast-off European clothes, they looked lost and harmless. This man was different. He was vital. Life and energy gleamed in his eyes. Gradually, as she unfroze from the paralyzing fear, she realized something else.

He was also stark naked.

Chapter 17

Sophie ran. She ran like her life depended upon it — not caring when her skirt caught on a prickly bush; not caring if a snake might be hidden in the grasses. Nothing scared her more than the man behind her.

She'd never seen a naked man before and hadn't really guessed what men looked like without clothes. A tiny part of her mind was trying to make sense of what she'd seen. Most of it, though, was figuring out what direction the church might be in. Eventually, of course, she got a pain in her side and was forced to stop to catch her breath. She listened hard, her heart thudding at every rustle in the trees, at every alarmed squawk from the birds. Before her body was ready to move, she listened to her fears and started stumbling down towards the harbour once more. When she stopped once more, she saw the sunlight dance along choppy waves, and ignoring the steepness of the hill, she ran towards the water. She fell, and her momentum tumbled her over a couple of logs. When she stopped, face downwards, her heart thudding and her lungs desperate for air, she wondered if she'd die.

After getting her breath back, Sophie huddled into the ground, trying to make herself as small as possible. She couldn't hear any noises suggesting that someone was hunting her, but that meant nothing. Native people everywhere depended upon their ability to stalk their prey quietly. Otherwise, they wouldn't eat. Soon, even the quietness became oppressive. Just as she decided to run again, she heard the thudding of horses' hooves in the distance, and she put her hands over the ears and huddled against the earth once more.

Faintly, somewhere in the distance, she heard her name. "Sophie? Sophie Mallory?" a child's voice shouted.

The horses seemed to be closer. Once again, she heard the boy's voice. "Sophie? Where are you?"

"Here!" she tried to shout, but her answer resembled a frog's croak. She gulped more air into her lungs, "Here!"

"She's near me, Polly," the child shouted. "I've found her."

"Sophie?" This time it was Polly's voice, faint but unmistakable. "Keep calling. We can't see you."

Sophie forced herself up. "Here! Can you hear me?"

She heard the sounds of a horse, then the child's excited voice. "Over here. I can see her, Polly."

Through the bushes, Sophie saw one of Polly's young brothers, James or John, on a horse twice his size. She'd met the twins briefly the night before, but couldn't tell which one was which. Before she could say anything, he wheeled his horse around to dash off in the opposite direction, presumably towards Polly.

"I'm here, Sophie," Polly called almost immediately. "Are you hurt?"

Sophie forced herself to move all her limbs. "No, I was just winded." She scrambled to her feet and stumbled out of the hollow towards the sound of Polly's voice. "Thank goodness you're here. We've got to help Luc. He's in the middle of a creek up there with a broken ankle."

"No, he's not. He's at home, sitting up, with a slightly sprained ankle. He's all right, Sophie. How do you think we knew where to look for you?"

"I don't believe it. He told me it was broken," Sophie answered, half relieved and half angry that all her efforts had been for nothing. Her terrible scare, her headlong dash down the hill. All for nothing. "Even so," she went on, after she'd thought for a bit, "how did he get back to Wahmurra?"

"Jimmy Bones," Polly answered briefly. "Come on, now. Think you can ride, if I lead Nance? There's a rock here you can use as a mounting block."

While Sophie settled herself on Nance, a huge — to her way of thinking — chestnut mare, Polly made a strange

163

call. "Coo-ee, coo-ee," she half-shouted, half-warbled. "She's fine. Go on back and let Lady Theodosia know."

Jimmy Bones, Sophie found out, was the medicine man for the natives in the area. Somehow, he and Lady Peter had formed a friendly partnership. He brought plants and dried roots and she gave him blankets and food. "He's very intelligent and friendly," she told Sophie later that morning. "I respect him. Next time, don't be so frightened."

"He doesn't wear clothes," Sophie said, somewhat indignantly.

"Not in the bush. But he always puts something on when he comes here. He knows we're not used to seeing people naked."

Sophie wasn't comforted. For the next couple of days, she stayed close to the main house. Even so, she enjoyed herself. There was so much to see. Workers made bricks in the brickyard from clay found on Wahmurra; sailors from places like China and Africa mended sails on the huge wharf. In many ways, Wahmurra was the same as some of the huge English estates she and Papa had visited. The difference, she found out, was that Wahmurra had to be self-sufficient. Although it imported a lot of household goods, such as plates and fabrics, they were luxuries. Except for certain pieces of machinery, everything else was Wahmurra-made.

One hot, sultry afternoon, everyone listlessly sat in the shade. Lady Theo and Lady Peter fanned themselves, James and John bickered between themselves, and no one else seemed to have any energy whatsoever. "I know what we should do," Polly said suddenly, looking at her brother. "Do you think you can manage to get to the cove, Billy?"

Billy tapped his crutches on the floor. "Why not?" Clumsily, he levered himself up from his chair. "Come on, Luc. It will be worth the effort. I promise."

"Is it all right, Mama?" Polly asked.

Lady Peter took a long time before she answered, and Sophie immediately wondered why she needed to think. "Yes, go ahead, dear."

Instead of going straight to the cove, wherever it was, Polly led the way to the bedrooms. "Change your clothes," she ordered. "Put on your oldest underwear and the dress you tore to bits the other day. Don't worry. Nobody will see you."

The cove, Sophie discovered, was a good ten minutes walk from the house. Two small headlands protected it from being seen from the wharf or the house. A small, sandy beach lay between the water and the cliff behind it, pockmarked by a couple of caves. A wooden platform with a ladder reaching down into the water floated on the waves about twenty yards from the shore. She could hear Billy and Luc somewhere, but couldn't see them.

"Come on," Polly ordered, as she headed to one of the caves.

Sophie followed, but was dumbstruck by what Polly did next. She took her dress off, as well as her boots and stockings. "Oh," she said, "I feel so much better."

Sophie looked at her. "What are you doing?"

"Nothing, yet. Come on, Sophie. Take your dress off. I'll help with your boots."

"What if someone sees us?" Sophie stammered, wondering if Polly had taken leave of her senses.

Polly didn't answer; she simply began to tug at Sophie's boots. When she'd finished, she took Sophie's dress in her hand and whipped it over her head. "No one will see us. Believe me."

Sophie felt ridiculously underdressed. "What about Luc and Billy? I can hear them."

"They're further down. Billy knows better than to come here, and I believe Luc is far too gentlemanly to try."

"Umph." Sophie certainly didn't know that. Nevertheless, she allowed Polly to tug her hand and lead her towards the water. "Don't go too far," she pleaded. "I can't swim."

"Not yet." Polly said.

For the next little while, Polly encouraged Sophie to lean back in the water, resting on her arm. "I won't let you drown. Just relax."

That was easier said than done. Sophie knew the water was only chest high, and that she could always put her feet down, but she still felt a little panicky, lying on top of it with only Polly's arm keeping her up. Gradually, she began to enjoy the sensation of drifting, and was almost lulled to sleep by the gentle waves rocking her back and forth. She opened her eyes, only to see Polly grinning at her from three feet away. She panicked, and immediately started to sink.

"Come on, Sophie. Stand up. I want to show you something else."

For the next hour or so, Sophie learned to float in the water, both on her face and her back. Polly even taught her how to stand on her hands — a trick she immediately wanted to show Luc. "It's so unfair," she wailed. "I finally learn something that he can't do and I can't show him. I don't even know if I can show Lady Theo. Maybe she'll think it indecent and forbid me to come here again."

"Oh, I've a fair idea that Mama will bring her here later tonight. Mama has firm ideas about people learning to swim if they live near the water. In a week or so, you'll be able to swim from here to the platform."

Sophie looked out to the platform. It seemed far away, but she was beginning to have confidence in Polly's confidence. "What's it for?" she asked, pointing to the platform.

"Mama had it built as a place for us to swim to so

that we could be better swimmers. But it's also for fun. Billy and I come here when it's hot and just jump off it into the water. James and John, as well. We'll make sure you learn to jump off it. That way, if a boat capsizes while you're on it in deep water, you'll know what to do."

That made sense. On the voyage out from England, Sophie had often wondered what she'd do if there were a shipwreck. Now she thought she'd have a chance of surviving it. Even as she smiled with satisfaction, a horn sounded three times from the direction of the main wharf.

"Out of the water," Polly ordered immediately. "Hurry."

Sophie obeyed, hurrying as best she could. "What's happening?" she gasped, running up the beach to the caves and her clothes.

"Sharks," Polly answered. "Let's hope Billy and Luc get out in time."

CHAPTER 18

From the safety of the small cave, Sophie watched two triangular fins streak through the water. "They're headed for Billy's cove," Polly exclaimed, pulling her dress over her head. "I hope he's paid attention to the horn."

Sophie hurriedly dressed and followed Polly as she ran towards the next cove. "Luc? Billy?"

"We see them," Billy shouted back. "Hey, look at that!"

Even from her spot on the rocks at water level, Sophie could see a sudden disturbance across the bay. "There's a school of fish there. It's dinner time for the sharks," Billy commented.

"That's one more lesson, Sophie. Sharks are extremely fast and can smell blood from miles away. If you've got a cut, make sure it's not bleeding if you go into the water."

The change from the fun of floating in the warm water to seeing fish gobbled up by sharks unsettled

Sophie. In the following days, she decided that the incident summed up Wahmurra. She remembered the
morning when she and Luke had gone for their stroll,
only to end up at a church service and her meeting of
Jimmy Bones. She loved going out on the water but,
it seemed, for every pleasure, there was also the threat
of danger.

Lady Peter insisted that everyone be taught to swim.
Even convicts were rewarded if they managed to thrash
their way from the platform to the beach. Sophie had
never met anyone quite like her. She seemed interested
in everyone and everything and served as Wahmurra's
unofficial doctor. In Lady Theo's world, sewing a fine
seam meant outstanding embroidery. In Lady Peter's
world, many men were grateful for the way she stitched
gaping wounds together with the finest of silk threads.
Lady Theo had the gift of making friends, and her
friendship was extended to Wynsham, Eloise, and John
Coachman. The men of Wahmurra, whether convicts or
free, would walk through bushfires for Lady Peter.

The two weeks they were supposed to spend at
Wahmurra flew by. On their last afternoon, Lady Theo
astounded Sophie. "Enjoy tonight," she told her. "It
will be your last free one for a while. When we get back
to Sydney, you'll be going to school with Polly."

Sophie felt like the air had been knocked right out of
her. She dropped on the nearby bamboo chaise like a stone
from a cliff. It was almost two years since she had been in a

proper school. During that time she had had governesses and shared Luc's tutor occasionally, but regular school had not been part of her life. "Where?" she asked.

"Mrs. Dixon's Seminary for Young Ladies of the Finest Respectability," Polly told her.

"You're lucky, then, Soph. They won't accept you," Luc hooted, appearing suddenly with Billy. "How could anyone call you 'a young lady of the finest respectability'?"

"Luc! Don't get too cocky, young man. You're off to Billy's school."

Polly danced around the room, her face alight with happiness. "Oh, Sophie. What fun. I hoped somehow Lady Theo would send you there so that we'd be together."

"And me?" Luc broke in, with an unhappy look on his handsome face. "Billy, your school's in Parramatta, isn't it? What's it like?"

Billy grimaced. "Like all schools, I suspect. Some boys hate King William's. For a while, so many ran away, they had to guard the bridges leading out of town. That was in Mr. Pine's day. He's gone now, and Mr. Spencer's the headmaster. He's a lot easier on our backsides, I can tell you."

Luc looked at Lady Theo. "I'll run away, too, if I don't like it."

"No doubt," she said dryly. "However, your brother agrees with me on this. It's King William's College for you."

"You'll like it. I promise," Billy told Luc, limping towards the door. "There's great swimming in the river, and Mr. Halden has us drill like soldiers. It's fun. I usually win the marksmanship medal, but I reckon you'll be giving me a run for my money. You're good."

Luc sat up, and Sophie thought that if he had been a bird, he would have preened his feathers. Such a small thing to make him like the school! Sometimes, boys were very strange. She turned to Polly to ask questions about Mrs. Dixon's school, but Lady Peter spoke. "Seeing it's the last night, I've asked Cook to put the food for a campfire in a basket. You four can grumble about schools to your heart's content, while the rest of us enjoy a more leisurely meal."

A campfire meal, Sophie discovered, was great fun. They hunted for branches and twigs and Billy built a great fire. After the flames died down, Polly showed Sophie how to cook her sausage on the end of a stick. It burnt, and the outside was black, but Sophie thought she'd never tasted anything better. Wahmurra's cook had excelled herself. There was newly made bread with jars of jams and fresh cream; cakes and pies; and fruit fresh from the vines and the orchard. Sophie had never tasted passion fruit before. She bit into the purple skin cautiously, and after an exploratory stab with her tongue, thoroughly enjoyed the taste.

"Papa had an important guest from England once," Polly told her. "Lord Somebody or other."

"Hodgkins," Billy told her.

"Whoever. Anyway, there was an emergency. We'd reached the fruit stage of the meal by then. Lord Hodgkins was really superior. All through the meal he'd kept telling us how much better things are in England, how much more elegant, and so on. Anyway, he got Billy's temper going, so Billy told him that the seeds were poisonous and couldn't be eaten. The poor man tried his hardest not to eat any. It was so funny."

Sophie grinned. Not eating passion fruit seeds would be like trying to isolate tomato seeds while eating the gooey stuff around them. It wouldn't pay to get on the wrong side of the Kendricks family. Both Billy and Polly would be fearsome enemies but great allies. Suddenly, Mrs. Dixon's Seminary for Young Ladies of the Highest Respectability didn't seem as scary.

"Is Mrs. Dixon's like all the other schools? What do you learn?"

"Well," Polly said as she crunched into a passion fruit, "it's not exactly like most schools in Sydney. It's not all music and manners. There's geography, English, French, and Italian," she went on, "arithmetic, and history — both natural and ancient. We've pretty decent teachers, but still, be sure you don't take harp lessons. Mr. Hughes is a fop of the highest order. Besides, they're twelve pounds extra."

"Don't worry. Playing the harp isn't one of my high ambitions. What are the girls like? They were awful at first when I went to school in England."

"Some are terrible. Their fathers have made a lot of money and they think everyone has to look up to them. You'll probably share a room with me and Mandy Johnson from Stroud. That's about thirty miles from here. She was with me at Governor Gipps' Garden Party."

Sophie didn't need to be reminded of that horrible occasion. "Is she pretty, with blond hair?"

"That's her," Polly said cheerfully. "She's as nice as she is pretty."

"Are any others nice?"

"I think you'll like some of the convict girls. They're called 'convict girls' even though it's their parents who were convicts, not them. They have to put up with a lot. Some girls are too high and mighty to talk to them. Others try to get them into trouble. Jemma Spruston's great. Nobody does nasty things to her, because she always gets them back. You'll like her. She's fun."

Lots of things in New South Wales were different. Even Billy and Polly themselves, come to think about it. And that reminded her: "Billy," she said. "What was the life and death thing you had to get to Wahmurra for the night you were attacked?"

"Yeah," echoed Luc, "I've been wondering about that. I know what I carried wasn't paper, but it was really light. What was in the package?"

There was a long silence. Sophie couldn't see Billy's face, but Polly's was hidden as she poked the fire with her stick. "We're not supposed to tell anyone," she muttered eventually. "We've promised."

"If you tell your secret, we'll tell you ours," Luc said with a slight laugh.

"Luc!" Sophie hissed, guessing what Luc had in mind. Even though she liked and trusted the Kendricks, she didn't know if she was prepared to bare her heart to them.

"What could be a bigger secret than your father's a convict who's engaged to marry one of the richest women in the Empire?" Polly said. "Maybe, it's that Luc's brother is a convict as well."

"Don't be silly, Polly."

"Well, it's true, after all. My brother is a convict and Sophie's my legally married wife."

"Pull another leg, Luc," Billy grinned. "I thought you'd come up with something really outlandish."

"This is outlandish," Luc told him. "I'm not joking. Sophie and I were married in March, 1839."

"That's impossible. Sophie would have been eleven, twelve at most," Polly asserted.

"Twelve," Sophie said. "It had to do with my brothers. First, they tried kidnapping me back to America. Then, they tried to get the courts to say that Lady Theo had no right to look after me. No one could find Papa because he'd lost his memory and couldn't tell anyone who he was. Luc married me so that I wouldn't have to go with my brothers."

Billy's mouth dropped open. "How old were you, Luc?"

"Fourteen."

"You can get married at fourteen?" Billy gave an exaggerated shiver before sitting up and turning to look at Luc. He whispered something and Sophie thought it sounded like, "Have you ... um?"

"Of course not," Luc muttered and turned away.

"Is the marriage legal here?"

"No," Sophie said emphatically, while Luc at the same time said, "Yes."

"That's probably the best answer," Luc said after looking over at Sophie. "Yes and no."

"I'll ask if we can tell you why Billy had to get home," Polly said. "It would be good to talk to someone about it."

The four of them sat quietly. The smoke kept the mosquitoes away, and although there were occasional rustlings in the bush, Sophie felt safe. She leaned back against a log and savoured the moment. She never imagined such contentment when she decided they had to follow Papa to New South Wales, and she was very thankful for it.

There was a movement on the edge of the clearing, and Polly reached over and grabbed her hand. When Sophie turned her head, Polly put a finger to her lips. Emboldened by the quietness, a couple of koalas ambled across the grass. As she watched them climb a tall gum tree, Sophie thought back to the conversation and absently wondered if she really was married. She didn't think so, but maybe she should ask Papa when she next saw him. Suddenly, she realized that might be difficult. "You board at school, don't you?" she burst out.

Billy and Polly looked puzzled. "Of course."

"When will I see Papa?" Sophie asked. "He won't be across the bay anymore."

Polly thought for a moment. "Lady Theo can arrange Sunday privileges for you. That way, she can pick you up in the morning and take you to Abbotsford."

"What about holidays?" Luc asked. "Are we allowed out for good behaviour?"

"Polly's supposed to get a fortnight in June and another in December," Billy answered. "King William's is a little more flexible. It's different for people who live in the country. Mama or Papa always say they need us. In any case, because Papa's a lord, people expect us to do things differently."

Maybe, Sophie thought. She was sure Mrs. Dixon, whoever she was, wouldn't be able to go against Lady Theo. Few people could. Maybe it would work out. Then she realized something else: Luc would be in Parramatta for eleven months of the year while she'd be in school-jail in Sydney. There'd be no more wild adventures.

Chapter 19

As the year of 1841 settled down, Sophie was proved right. There were no new adventures, for either Luc or herself — unless, of course, she counted school as one. After being so close to Luc and Lady Theo, she felt the separation from them as badly as that from Papa. The only consolation was Visiting Sundays. John Coachman picked her up promptly after church and drove her to Abbotsford. Usually Luc managed leave, or an *exeat*, then as well.

The last Sunday in August, Sophie and Luc sat near a roaring fire in the blue salon, warming their hands and catching up on each other's news. Cousin Mary had worked her decorating magic so that, even in the dead of winter, the room managed to look warm and welcoming.

"King William's really is the best school, Soph. If I have to go to school at all, it's the one."

"I thought it was horrible. One of the girls in my class had a brother there who ran away."

"A bolter. That's what we call runaways."

"He told Jemma there was a kind of chair and you had to lean against it when you were whipped."

Luc shrugged, his own individual shoulder movement that Sophie now realized she loved. "Yeah. There's the flogging stool. Never tried it myself, though."

Sophie thrust the thought of him being whipped out of her mind with difficulty. Luc could go off in so many directions, it was a wonder he'd fitted into the school and its way of doing things. "What do you like particularly about King William's?"

"The lessons. I'm ahead of everyone in Greek, thanks to old Toplofty in Montreal. I know geography better because I've been around the world, except for the Pacific Ocean, so it makes sense for me."

"Me too," Sophie told me. "I'm head of the school in geography, and I think it's for the same reason. Everything makes sense. Well, sort of."

They talked about school and realized, to their great delight, that the King William's students were invited to the Grand Ball put on by Mrs. Dixon. "Polly says Mrs. Dixon usually asks the boys from Sydney College, but, because so many arrived drunk last year, she's asking another school. We haven't been told which one yet. I can't wait to tell Polly."

"She'll know," Luc answered briefly. "Billy went

home this weekend as well. He said .... Ah, there's Marc. I can hear his tread."

"And Papa!" Sophie exclaimed, jumping to her feet and rushing to the door. "Come in here. It's warm."

Both Papa and Marc looked worse than they had in the summer. Their faces were grey and they seemed gaunt. However, their smiles were as exuberant as ever, and Papa swung Sophie into his arms for a hug. "Hey," he said, holding her at arms' length. "You're growing up on me. I like your hair this way."

Sophie blushed. She had only recently begun to wear her curls in a loose knot on top of her head. "I'm only allowed to do this on Sundays or special occasions. Mrs. Dixon's pretty strict about how we look."

Luc reached over and casually patted it. "Looks like a bird's nest to me," he said casually. When Sophie didn't hit him in response, he looked shocked. "My. You really are becoming a lady. What was it? A 'Young Lady of the Highest Respectability'?"

This time Sophie punched his arm. "Almost," she said, grinning. "Not quite."

"Sophie!" Lady Theo exclaimed as she entered the room. "I thought you'd grown out of that."

"Never," Luc answered. "Not in a million years." His eyes lightened as he saw Wynsham, Cousin Mary, and Cook coming in with trays of refreshments. "Oh," he went on, closing his eyes and lifting his head dramatically. "Heaven. I dream of your cakes, Cookie."

After he had demolished one entire tray, Marc looked at him affectionately before speaking. "We have news. Good and bad, I'm afraid. Poor Ignace Chèvrefils has gone to the Sydney Hospital. It looks bad."

Lady Theo looked sad. "He looked half starved when I last saw him."

"He was," Papa told her angrily. "The government's to blame. It pays for good food, but nobody checks that we actually get it. Baddeley and his friends sell everything. If one of our men wasn't the cook, I swear our soup would be made out of dirt. That's exactly what the flour he has to make bread with looks like, except that it has hundreds of weevils running around in it. If it wasn't for your gardens, Theo, and those of our kind neighbours, I think all of us would be sick like Ignace."

"Will he die?" Sophie asked.

Marc nodded. "He looks exactly like Rochon did when they took him to the hospital, and he never returned. Ignace is the tallest of all of us, and he's just not getting enough food. I'd like to see Baddeley live on our rations. He'd be casting up his accounts in five minutes, I tell you."

The news saddened everyone. Chèvrefils used the Longbottom wharf regularly, and during the summer, it had been easy to slip him some contraband food. Sophie absently rearranged some of Cousin Mary's flowers while she tried to expel thoughts of her father starving to death from her mind. "You said you had good news," she said to Marc. "What was it?"

"I've been assigned, together with nineteen others. We're supposed to leave Longbottom about Wednesday or so."

"I've heard that rumour before," Lady Theo said dryly.

Sophie nodded. "It's cruel. All these rumours. They make you hope, and then, nothing happens."

That was true. The convicts at Longbottom had been plagued by rumours of getting out for months. Sometimes it seemed people said they'd heard of assignments just to make them happy. The rumours about them were everywhere.

"Oh, they're true, this time. I've seen my papers. I'm going to a wine merchant — Monsieur Joubert of Hunter's Hill," Marc told everyone.

"Maybe," Papa contributed. "Don't forget what happened to Provost. He was assigned to Mr. Brown in Parramatta. He was supposed to get twenty pounds a year and free clothing. When he arrived, Mr. Brown told him he'd changed his mind. He said he could get free people for fifteen pounds and *they* provided their own clothes."

"Well, yes. But can they work as well as we do? That's the question."

"Lepailleur told me that Mr. Neich is going to ask for him," Luc contributed.

"Well, if anyone knows what the Canadians are like, it's him," Wynsham said suddenly from the corner. Sophie must have looked puzzled, for he went on, "Mr. Neich is the owner of the Bath Arms. Remember? You met him when you first arrived."

As Sophie nodded, Luc laughed. "Do you know what the funniest thing about Neich is? He shouldn't even be here in the first place. He's Italian. When he was younger, he wanted to see something of the world, so he travelled to France, and then, somehow, ended up in Africa. One morning, he was hung over and homesick, so he wandered down to the docks and looked at the notices saying where the ships there were headed for. One said Holland. 'Holland,' he thinks to himself, 'I can easily get home from there,' so he pays his passage." Luc stopped, enjoying the gasps from his audience and Wynsham's chuckle.

"Like I said," he went on, "poor Neich had drunk too much wine. He kept to his cabin for a few days, telling the steward he had the *mal de mer*. Eventually, his 'sea-sickness' went away and he went up on deck. After a while, he worked out that the ship was sailing south. When he asked why, he found out that it was going to *New* Holland, to New South Wales, not old Holland in Europe. He came, liked the place, and, end of story."

Everyone laughed. Sophie couldn't imagine getting on a ship and not knowing exactly where it was going. She hoped Mr. Neich would be able to get Maurice

Lepailleur assigned to him. Lepailleur was a good man and deserved a good employer. "What about you, Papa? Do you know where you're going?"

"Not yet. When we last saw the Kendricks, Lord Peter said that, although the competition for the Canadians was high, he thought he might get five of us. He didn't specifically ask for me, he said. He thought it would be easier to ask for men with woodcutting experience."

"So, you don't know where you'll end up?"

Papa shook his head. "The first nineteen go out this week, though. That seems certain. Maybe I'll be in the next nineteen."

By the time of Sophie's November Visiting Sunday, little had changed. Poor Chèvrefils had indeed died, and that blighted everyone's spirits. Sophie cheered herself up by going for a quick sail out in the harbour, but really didn't enjoy it. She was worried about Papa, and the sting of the sea waves against her cheeks seemed like slaps from fate. Surely, she thought, with Lord Peter and Lady Theo's influence behind him, Papa should have been assigned.

"Lord Peter thinks it's good news, actually," Lady Theo said after she returned and they waited for Papa. "He thinks there's a chance that Benjamin will go straight through to the ticket-of-leave status."

"That means he could work anywhere," Sophie said, smiling at the thought of her father finally getting out of Longbottom.

"It also means that we can finally marry," Lady Theo told her. "Of course, it will be three years later than we thought. Maybe we'll be able to have a December 1841 wedding instead of the December '38 one we planned."

"We'd better hope another rebellion doesn't break out," Sophie told her. "Do you have any more news? Has King William's kicked Luc out yet?"

"No, the headmaster told me they're very happy with Luc. Apparently, he's shown good leadership."

Sophie snorted. "Him? I wonder what he's planning."

"No, Sophie. He was here last Sunday, and he really likes the school. It has a mixture of outdoor things that he loves and good teaching. He's a sergeant in their drill corps. As well, he's the top student in his class. Mr. Spencer says he thinks Luc could get a scholarship to Oxford if he tried."

Sophie tried to put this Luc into the picture of the one she knew. She'd always known he was clever, but not that he was academically brilliant. She could understand him being promoted to sergeant easily. That fitted with everything she knew. The Luc who might get a scholarship to Oxford didn't.

Cousin Mary waltzed into the room. As usual, she looked ethereally beautiful. Sophie could never work out what made her so. The right side of her face was slightly wider than the left; her nose was tilted to one side. Still, her smile was dazzling and she always seemed to warm up a room simply by being in it. "I saw Cousin Benjamin on the dock," she told Lady Theo. "He should be here any moment."

A couple of moments later, Papa walked into the room. He kissed Lady Theo and hugged Sophie. "Any more news?" Lady Theo asked as Wynsham followed with the silver teapot and three cups and saucers.

"Oh, a couple more men are supposed to go on Wednesday," he said almost wearily.

"Not Benjamin Mallory, I assume," Lady Theo responded.

He shook his head. "The waiting is getting on everyone's nerves. We know that we'll be going soon, but where and when is what we worry about. It's all the men think about, talk about. There's even a betting pool going with a kind of reverse prize. Everyone puts a penny into a box every week. The last man to be assigned gets the pot."

"That's not much of a prize," Sophie told him. "I think I'd rather be the first one out."

"It's hard on everyone. Baddeley and his friends are like snarling dogs. They're losing their workers and some of their income. Worse, you know how we've talked about Baddeley being mad? I think it might actually be true. He's so erratic that no one will go near him. The other day a branch came down in a storm and he ordered a whipping for all the men in the nearest hut. Fortunately, everyone dithered and dallied, and he forgot all about it."

"Fortunately, indeed," Wynsham said as he refilled Sophie's teacup.

"How's Mr. Lepailleur doing?" Sophie asked. "Is he at Mr. Neich's yet?"

"No. He's going crazy as well, in his own way. He writes about his family in his journal all the time. Just last week his youngest son turned four, and Lepailleur sobbed because he couldn't be there to give him a present. He says he dreams about his wife every night. He's just at the point of putting his arms around her when he wakes up."

"Poor man. It's not right that he's away from his wife for so long," Cousin Mary asserted strongly. "I know how I'd feel."

For a second, Sophie saw a strange look on Wynsham's face. Immediately, she thought of Miriam Peters at Mrs. Dixon's. She wore the same kind of look every time Billy Kendricks was talked about. She quickly turned towards Cousin Mary, but her face was as placid as usual, and when she looked back at Wynsham, his face was expressionless. She wanted to tell Polly and Luc her suspicions. Wynsham and Cousin Mary? What would the great Earl Bentleigh think about that?

CHAPTER 20

As though she had conjured them up, there was a clatter in the hallway and seconds later Wynsham ushered Marc and Luc into the room. "We've got great news," Luc proclaimed happily.

And so have I, Sophie thought as she squeezed up to allow Luc to sit next to her on the settee.

"What's the news, Marc?" Papa asked.

"The best, I think. Lord Peter came to our shop yesterday and bought ten cases of wine. He explained to Monsieur Joubert they were to be a wedding present. His wife's best friend was getting married at Christmas. He asked if I would be allowed to take the wine to Wahmurra at Christmas time, and even offered to reimburse him for my wages. Congratulations, Ben."

Both Papa and Lady Theo looked puzzled, Sophie noted. She dug Luc in the ribs and whispered, "Whose wedding?"

"Your Papa's and Lady T's, of course."

"How is this possible?" Papa asked Marc. "It's nothing but another horrible rumour."

"No. It's not. Your assignment papers went to Longbottom ages ago, apparently. Who knows if Maddeley Baddeley truly mislaid them or lost them on purpose? Anyway, according to Lord Peter, Major Barney himself is coming here tomorrow. You were assigned to Lord Peter, along with Guimond and Basile Roy. Yours weren't the only papers that were lost. Because of this, Major Barney's decided that everyone should become ticket-of-leave men. Lord Peter has your paperwork. You'll be free tomorrow, Ben. Me, within a month or so, I expect."

Papa sat down on the nearest chair, one of Lady Theo's cherished Sheratons. "I simply can't believe it. I can't afford to put trust in another rumour, Marc. It hurts too much when they don't come true."

Lady Theo walked across to Papa and held on to his hands. "It must be true, Ben. There are too many details for this to be a rumour. But what's this about a wedding?"

Marc looked a little abashed. "I think Lord and Lady Peter are coming here tomorrow, and that this was to be their big surprise. The wedding's to be their present. I think you must have told them you'd like to be married at Wahmurra — at least, that's what I understand."

After this, everyone talked at once. Papa and Lady

Theo were the quietest. They sat together, hand in hand, and smiled. Sophie and Luc bombarded Marc with questions. How were they going to get to Wahmurra? Would they be able to get out of school early?

"Tomorrow," Marc laughed as he held up his hands to stop the question barrage. "Ask Lord Peter tomorrow. I think he and Lady Peter have it all planned."

"Oh. Lady Theo, can I be late back to school? Could John tell Mrs. Dixon I'm sick or something, and that I'll be back on Tuesday?"

"I'll go," Cousin Mary volunteered. "I want to buy some new material for the curtains in your room, Theo. I can kill two birds with the one stone."

"And have an excuse to be out of the way when Lord Peter calls," Luc muttered to Sophie, only to sit up with his back as straight as a ramrod when Lady Theo looked at him.

Sophie spent the following morning on the river, paddling to all her favourite places and searching for a glimpse of the Kendricks's sloop. It was hard work, and her muscles protested every time she dug the paddle into the waves. She returned for lunch discouraged, only to find that the Kendricks had come by carriage and Lady Peter was ensconced in the Blue Parlour. Lady Theo was twittering and a fascinated Sophie stared at her. She fiddled with the flower arrangements, idly dusted the Meissen pottery dog with her handkerchief, arranged and rearranged her pearls.

"Don't fret, Theo," Lady Peter told her. "Peter didn't guarantee that they'd be able to get here for lunch."

"There's a chance, Christina. A chance to eat a meal with Benjamin and celebrate that he's finally out of that place," she retorted, getting up and pacing around the room.

Sophie fled. If Papa and Lord Peter were expected, she wanted to look her best for the celebration. She tried on a few dresses and found they were either too short or too tight. She sighed. Obviously, she'd be spending the next few weeks getting outfitted, once again, by Mrs. Halladay. Walking across to the window which looked out towards Longbottom, she searched for signs of Papa with the same intensity as she'd looked for the sloop earlier. Would Baddeley have the audacity to keep Papa there until the last possible moment?

Probably. How anxious Papa must be, wondering if his release would be a mirage or not. They had to do something to really celebrate when he walked through the door, she decided, and she ran downstairs to consult Wynsham. If at all possible, Papa would have their equivalent of a nine-gun salute.

Organizing this kept her busy as the minutes ticked by. When the under-groom ran up to breathlessly announce that Papa and Lord Peter were on their way, everything was ready. As a startled Papa and Lord Peter walked into the house, Sophie popped the cork of the first champagne bottle, then Lady Theo, Lady Peter, Wynsham, Cook,

Eloise, Maggie, Sophie, and Lady Theo again.

Papa's wide smile said his thanks.

If time had dragged for most of 1841, the last month flew by in a blur. Sophie finished her year at Mrs. Dixon's, receiving first prize in Geography at the Prize Giving. She even thought she might miss the friendship of some girls. She wouldn't see Jemma or Miriam until school recommenced, but Mandy Johnson promised to come across to Wahmurra from her home in Stroud.

Lady Theo had moved to Double Bay, and Cousin Mary's talents were making the house a showpiece. When Sophie arrived, she couldn't believe that Cousin Mary had been able to put her dreams into reality. The wallpaper in her bedroom perfectly matched the bed's counterpane and gave it an airy, fresh atmosphere. She had only a couple of days to appreciate it, though, before she, Lady Theo, and Polly and her mother left for Wahmurra on the sloop.

All the men, including Luc, rode up the next day. From their conversation, after they arrived, Sophie gathered that they spent much of the time watching for possible bushranger attacks on the luggage coaches they escorted. Apparently, the whole area between the Hawkesbury River to Taree, a town north of Wahmurra, was abuzz with the news that the colony's most infamous convict had escaped from the Maitland jail and was preying on travellers.

Papa and Lady Theo were married in the church down by the creek, with Preacher Dan assisting the Wahmurra chaplain. Marc was Papa's best man, and Sophie was Lady Theo's maid of honour. Mrs. Halladay had made a simple dress of a pale gold and Sophie felt joyful as she watched Papa and Lady Theo pledge themselves to each other. She barely remembered her own ceremony. At the time, she had been frightened that someone would find out about it and stop it. As well, part had been in French, and she hadn't understood it. All she truly remembered was that although both she and Luc had concentrated on making their "I dos" loud, they hadn't really looked at each other. When Preacher Dan told Papa he might kiss Lady Theo, Sophie took a fast look back at Luc. To her surprise, he was looking at her and she didn't understand the expression on his face, but she knew somehow that he was also remembering the frantic morning they married in Montreal.

Lord Peter lent his sloop for a month-long honeymoon, and Papa and Lady Theo left the following morning. Sophie had almost cried when she said goodbye. "I know I can't with go with you," she told Lady Theo. "That doesn't stop me from wishing I could. It will be the first time since Montreal that I've been without you."

Lady Theo ignored her new dress and pulled Sophie close for a real hug. "Silly," she told her, wiping the tears away with a handkerchief. "You've been at school all year. Away from me for weeks at a time. Your Papa and I need this time alone, child. It's been years since we had such an opportunity. Be happy for us."

"I am happy for you," Sophie protested. "It's just that I can't shake this feeling of danger."

"Pooh," Lady Theo retorted inelegantly. "Think about it. What could happen? Even if the sloop capsized, I know how to swim now, thanks to Lady Peter. When we come back, I'll ask Mrs. Dixon to let you out of school for a week. Then, you and I will begin again. I'm your Mama now and I promise to take good care of you."

When Papa appeared a minute or so later, Sophie couldn't remember him looking so happy. She stood on the Wahmurra wharf a little later with Luc and the entire Kendricks family to wave goodbye, but the feeling of danger didn't go away. *God*, she prayed silently, *keep them safe*.

CHAPTER 21

Several days later, Sophie, Polly, Billy, and Luc left Wahmurra for school. Sophie and Polly would arrive a week late, a fact that caused them great happiness. Mr. White, the overseer, and four Wahmurra men escorted them, as he had business in Parramatta and in Maitland on his way back.

On the stretch of road heading south from Maitland, Polly turned to Sophie. "It's times like this I want to be a boy. Look at them all," she exclaimed, pointing to Luc, Billy, and Mr. White riding alongside their coach. "They don't get their bones shaken to bits every time we go over a pothole. They have the breeze in their faces, and, of course, they can canter off any time they jolly well like. We're prisoners in here."

Sophie didn't feel so disgruntled. She could hold her own on horseback on city streets or in a demure trot in a city park, but riding for eight or nine hours at a time would have been a hardship. Still, she was grateful for every break in the journey, and ready for bed once they'd reached Wiseman's Ferry. The next morning they left the four Wahmurra men behind to wait for Mr. White's return and took the first ferry across the Hawkesbury River.

Each mile they travelled down the Great Northern Road not only brought them closer to Sydney, but also to Pennant Hills and the road to Parramatta. There, after lunch at an inn, Billy and Luc said their goodbyes and headed west towards King William's. Sophie and Polly had little to say, and Sophie imagined that Polly felt as she did: like a valuable part of her had just left.

The first sign that something was wrong came when the coach slowed to a crawl. "One of the horses has lost his shoe," Mr. White reported. "We'll have to stop at the nearest smithy. There's probably one in Ryde."

Polly groaned. "That's probably all there is. Isn't there one at Kissing Point? We could explore the river while we wait."

By nursing the horse along, it took an hour to reach the smithy. Mr. White talked to the blacksmith, and by his reaction, Sophie knew the news was bad. "There's two people ahead of us. He says it will be another hour, at least, before he can start."

"We don't mind," Polly said, jumping down from the coach. "It will be wonderful to stretch our legs. Come on, Sophie."

"I have to be in Sydney in time to eat dinner at Government House," Mr. White replied. "It's important."

"Can you still get there in time?" Polly asked, looking towards the setting sun in the west.

"If I catch the next ferry across and ride like the dickens," Mr. White replied, after checking his pocket watch.

"Well, do it," Polly told him. "Sophie and I can get to school at any time. It doesn't matter if we're late. We'll stay in sight of the smithy and Jim can come get us when everything's finished."

Mr. White looked worried. "I suppose you will be all right. I'll tell Jim to keep a strict eye on you. Promise you won't wander? You, as well, Miss Sophie."

After he left, Sophie and Polly walked to the river's edge. Sophie was in familiar territory. She had often paddled her canoe across the river to the Kissing Point area, and as she peered into the distance, she imagined she could see their house at Abbotsford.

"It's almost like a year ago," she told Polly, who was balancing on some rocks. "If I close my eyes, I can imagine paddling home from here."

"Your home is in Double Bay," Polly told her, a smile on her face. "We'll go there together on Visiting Sundays now."

"Hmm," Sophie replied absently. She knew the long hours she had spent on the river would always be somehow associated with the word "home," just as Malloryville in Vermont and London would be. Polly wouldn't understand. She hadn't moved around like Sophie had.

The sun had long set when Jim pulled the horses up in front of Mrs. Dixon's school. Usually, gaslight blazed from the ground floor. Tonight, however, there seemed to only be a light or two in the back rooms. The second floor, as well, was suspiciously dark.

"Do you have the right address?" Polly asked.

"Of course. I've been bringing you here for years. I know which house is which," Jim replied. When he opened the door of the coach, Sophie saw how worried he was. "I'll try to find out what's happened," he said, walking towards the front door.

"Well, here's a turn-up for the books," he said when he came back a few minutes later. "One of the girls returned after Christmas with scarlet fever. The school's in quarantine."

"Polly," a voice called from the darkened second floor.

Both Sophie and Polly climbed out of the coach and stared at the building. As soon as their eyes adjusted, they saw several pale faces staring down at them. "Mandy?" Polly called back.

"Polly, can you get us out of here? No one's sick in our room, and we're deathly scared that we'll catch the fever."

"What's happened?" Sophie asked.

"It's one of the new girls. She looked like she'd been out in the sun too much. I met her the first day, and now they won't let me leave. They say I'm contagious."

"You probably are," Polly answered grimly, and Sophie wished they could help. Scarlet fever was a terrible illness, and the odds were that Mandy would succumb to it. "Is your throat sore?"

"No," Mandy answered and sounded indignant. "I haven't any rashes, either."

"None of us have," another girl said, half-hanging out the window in her desire to get out. "Can't you take us home?"

Polly looked at the girls and shook her head. Sophie thought that if Mrs. Dixon didn't prune the ivy so that it didn't grow higher than the ground-floor windows, the girls would have climbed down it in their eagerness to get away from their peril. "Do you need food?"

"No, they're feeding us. Probably fattening us up before we die," Mandy said bitterly.

Sophie looked at Polly. "Can we do anything?"

Polly shook her head again. "Mandy, there's one thing you can do: make sure they keep your cups and plates, knives and forks separate from the sick girls' things. Tell them to always wash them in boiling water. That's the best way to avoid getting sick. That's what Mama would say."

The girls inside the house pulled back from the windows for a moment, and Sophie saw them talking amongst themselves. Mandy came back to the window. "I say, Polly. Is Lady Peter in town? Could you ask her for help?"

"She's at Wahmurra."

The horses stamped their feet, seemingly eager to leave the desolate school. "Where to now?" Jim asked. "I reckon the horses have one last trip left in them."

Sophie looked at Polly, who seemed lost in thought. "Abbotsford," she directed, making the decision for her friend. "You can leave your horses there and take fresh ones."

Polly came to life. "That's a good idea. Besides, Abbotsford's closer to Wahmurra. We'll have to send a messenger to let Mama know."

"No need for that, Miss Polly. I'll tell Mr. White."

"Well, make sure Mama knows, although I can't see what she can do."

As the coach turned and began trundling its way back to Abbotsford, both Sophie and Polly were silent. Only after they had left the city proper did Polly give a hint of what she was thinking. "I wonder if we'll ever come back. There's no telling what kind of financial disaster this is for Mrs. Dixon. She will have to refund all our fees, feed those who are sick, supply them with doctors and medicines, and probably pay the wages of our teachers. She might go into bankruptcy. It's happened to other schools."

"I hope not, I've been happy there," Sophie responded. If she had to go to school at all, Mrs. Dixon's school was all right. She would be sorry if it closed. "How long will it be before the quarantine's removed?" she asked Polly.

"Three weeks, maybe four. They'll want to make sure that everyone is well before they can open it again. Scarlet fever is a horrible disease. I really hope no one dies from it. I almost did."

For a while she stared out the window, wondering how they could help. Then, as the carriage turned onto the Parramatta Road, she realized what Polly had said. "You had scarlet fever? Was it horrible?"

"Oh, yes. Everyone thought I would die. Mama and Papa were down here, and as I was only five, Billy and I were still at Wahmurra. We had a young convict then called Thad. He and a friend rode down here and convinced Mama to come home. The friend was almost killed. It was touch and go for a while for both of us."

Despite the dangers she'd faced, Sophie's recent experiences had never been life-threatening. She didn't quite know how to react. "Do you think anyone will die?"

Polly looked sad. "Oh, yes. One or two. Maybe more. Nobody quite knows how to treat it."

"Maybe we should ask John Coachman to take us back to Wahmurra and ask your mama to come down. If we go with Cousin Mary, it would be quite proper."

"That's a great idea, and better yet, John might only have to take us as far as Wiseman's Ferry. We could catch up with Mr. White."

Buoyed by this plan, Sophie sat back against the cushions, watching the miles go by. Soon, she began to recognize landmarks. "There's the Bath Arms," she told Polly. "I wonder if Maurice Lepailleur is working there. Surely, he must be out of Longbottom by now."

"Here we are," Polly remarked in reply. "It feels funny arriving by road and not by water. I don't think I've ever come this way before."

Sophie took a moment to survey the house once they had reached its driveway. It was hard to remember her first impressions of it. Almost a year ago, it had been dilapidated, with gaping holes in its roof. The gardens had been a morass of weeds, and the fruit trees had had branches shooting off in all directions. Now, the house was a showpiece. Its doors and shutters were painted white, its brass knocker and door handles gleamed with polish, and the gardens were beautiful. Even the orchard had been tamed. Luc and his fellow owners could count on getting a sizeable return from their investment.

After the groom brought the carriage to a halt in front of the door, Sophie jumped out without waiting for his help and rapped on the door impatiently. Wynsham must be in the cellars or something, she thought, as minutes went by without it being opened.

"Wynsham's taking his time, isn't he?" Polly said.

Sophie rapped louder. "He mustn't be able to hear. I'll try again."

The door flew open almost immediately, and Sophie stared at the woman in the doorway. She was smallish, about Sophie's own height. But that was the only resemblance. Her greying hair was pulled back into a tight bun, although wisps of hair had managed to escape and fluttered defiantly in the breeze. The woman's eyes were brown and as beady as those of a magpie. Sophie thought they had the same expression of one of the more manic ones, the kind who swooped down whenever people went near their particular tree. Her puffy cheeks were red and her mouth an angry thin line. She seemed to be almost skin and bones, but Sophie detected strength in her upright body. Her clothes were drab and colourless. Sophie thought her dress might have been a pewter-grey at some time. The only colour she had, apart from her red cheeks, was a pristine white apron.

"Who are you?" Sophie asked.

"Me?" the woman spat out. "More to the point, who are you? Another Jezebel and her friend, I assume."

"Where's Wynsham?"

"Frying in hell," was the disconcerting reply.

Sophie tried to enter the house. The woman immediately blocked the doorway.

"Don't be stupid. Let me in," Sophie snapped. "What right have you got to stop me? Who are you, anyway?"

"I've every right to prevent Lady Thornleigh of being taken advantage of again. I realize it's happened once, but not again. Not while I can help it."

"She's a madwoman, Soph. She must have escaped from the asylum in Tarban Creek and crossed the river somehow. Let's go round the back and find out from Cook what's happening."

Sophie turned back to look at the woman. Polly might be right, she thought. The woman was obviously insane. She decided to make one last attempt. "Who are you?" she asked once more. "Would you mind telling me your name?"

"No mystery about it, and I'm not a lunatic. Although, from some of the things I've heard, I wonder about this household." She drew herself up to her full height of five foot three and poked Sophie in the chest with her right index finger. "I don't know who you are, young madam, but I am Lady Thornleigh's cousin. I'm Mrs. Vickery."

"Cousin Mary," Sophie breathed, and she felt like laughing hysterically.

CHAPTER 21

Rather than deal with the angry Mrs. Vickery, Sophie tugged Polly towards the kitchen. To her relief, Cook had her hands in a huge mixing bowl, kneading dough for bread. "Miss Sophie," she exclaimed. "Thank goodness you're here. As soon as I finish baking this bread, I'm out of here. I quit."

"What on earth's going on? Who is that woman?" The questions burst out like air from the dough.

Cook kept her hands moving, but her face was wrinkled with worry. "*She* says she's her ladyship's cousin and was supposed to come out here with you. Instead, she got sick and had to wait all this time until was she better."

Sophie watched Cook pound the dough a little more savagely as she spoke. She understood. A year was a long time to convalesce. Even if the illness had been nearly fatal, the woman would have had six months on a ship to regain her health. Her story sounded fishy. Poor Cook.

"Where's Wynsham?"

Cook stopped pounding for a moment, and smiled. "On his honeymoon. Her ladyship approved it. He married Mary, and it was ever so beautiful. She looked just like an angel, her dress was so lovely."

That was the first thing that had made sense. If Cousin Mary, or whoever she was, married, she would have made sure that her dress was exquisite. "When will they be back?" Polly asked, a grin on her face as she thought of all the explanations that would have to be made.

"Next week," Cook said, pounding the dough furiously. "Until then, I have to put up with madam in there," she jerked her head towards the front of the house, "by myself. That's why I quit. John's no good. Takes himself off whenever he can. Like today. He's gone to Parramatta. Anywhere, to get out of range of that tongue."

"Who is she really, do you know?" Sophie asked.

Cook sniffed. "Probably who she says. All of us knew early on that the other Mrs. Vickery wasn't, if you know what I mean. Earlier than you lot did, I can assure you. Our Mrs. Vickery only came here when she found out that that one," she pointed again to the front with her thumb, "wasn't going to take her ladyship's brother up on his offer. She worked in the same house as her. That's how she knew about it. It was probably stealing in a way, but her ladyship laughed when Wynsham confessed everything to her. 'The last thing Sydney needs is another convict,' she told him. She said she'd had good value from young Mary and they could marry with her blessing."

"Ah," Sophie said, as she understood so many things.

"But what's going to happen now?" Polly asked. "I don't want to stay here with that woman, thank you very much."

"Me, either," Sophie answered with determination. She thought for a moment, and galvanized into action. "Polly, see if you can catch Jim before he leaves. I've an idea."

After Polly left the kitchen, she looked at Cook. "I think the best thing you could do, in these circumstances, is to have John Coachman take you and your stuff here over to Double Bay. You can tell Mrs. Vickery that I think the house there is ill-prepared for Lady Theo's return. That should put you out of harm's way. If she says she wants to go as well, remind her that she's needed here to keep an eye on everyone. John can stay here or with you. That will be up to him."

Cook beamed. "I'll just finish baking the bread and get everything together. You're a good girl, Miss Sophie. Thank you. But what will you do?"

Polly raced back into the kitchen. "Phew. Mrs. Vickery almost managed to catch me. But I didn't catch Jim. He'd already left. What did you want him for?"

"I wanted him to ask Mr. White to collect us on his way back to Wahmurra tomorrow," Sophie answered.

"I'd rather be there than anywhere close to that woman until Lady Theo comes back or Mrs. Dixon sends for us. What do you think?"

"I think that if we get an early start, we could be on our way before SHE wakes up. We'd only have to go to Wiseman's Ferry and wait there for Mr. White. So, I say we wait here until she goes to bed, then creep upstairs. We can always sleep in the carriage."

Sophie nodded. It made sense. But, when she went out to the stables, she encountered problems. It seemed that the under-groom had quit after a run-in with the new Cousin Mary. "I would have quit too," the stable-boy told her. "But I've got nowhere else to go."

"Can you drive a team?" Sophie asked.

The boy gulped. "Yes, as long as John Coachman is with me."

"What's your name?"

"Tim," he replied, looking at his muddy boots.

"Then listen to me, Tim," Sophie said and went on to explain that they needed the carriage ready to leave just after breakfast. "If John Coachman doesn't come back, you'll have to take us to Wiseman's Ferry. Do you know the way?"

"Up the Great Northern Road. You take the Kissing Point ferry."

"Good." Satisfied that he understood, Sophie walked slowly towards the kitchen. She smiled as she thought of Cousin Mary's courage, then frowned as she considered the new Cousin Mary and wondered how Lady Theo would handle her, wishing she could be a fly on the wall during their first meeting.

Although Tim had the carriage ready in time, he was clearly nervous and unhappy. "Will you leave a note for John Coachman telling him that you made me take you?" he asked, and still looked unhappy after Sophie gave him a written note.

That was the first delay. Next, Cook asked whether or not she should pack the china and silverware for transfer to Double Bay, and she kept adding more and more food to their lunch basket. They missed the first ferry across the river by seconds and had to wait half an hour. Next, Sophie noticed that for every mile they put between them and Abbotsford, Tim drove a little slower and slower. Even when the road was clear, he kept the same easy pace.

"We'll be lucky if we get there by midnight," Polly grumbled.

"Or tomorrow," Sophie said. "I dare not say anything to him. If he gets any more nervous, he'll spook the horses. Let's change the subject. Do you think this Mrs. Vickery is the real Cousin Mary? I like the other one much better."

"Well, it certainly explains why Papa's never met her," Polly laughed.

"Yes. It all makes sense now. She must have hidden every time a stranger came, in case the stranger could identify her. That's why she didn't leave her room when

209

Billy first came, why she hated going visiting and paying calls with Lady Theo."

"And why she can't read," Polly added.

Sophie looked at her in surprise as the horses began the slow climb to Glenorie Heights. The air was cooler, and every now and then they heard the sweet sound of a bellbird. "How did you know about that?"

"Oh, Billy worked it out. He thought when Lady Theo sent her in to read to him, it was like a test. Cousin Mary had all kinds of ways of disguising it. She'd ask Billy where Lady Theo or you had left off, and they'd try to figure out what might happen next. Then, her time would be up and she'd scamper out the door. He said he made all kinds of games up to try to force her to read, but she avoided all his efforts."

"And ours as well." Sophie laughed and told Polly some of the things she and Luc had done. By the time she had finished, she looked out the window and found the carriage just about at the top of the Glenorie hills. "Hey, look, Polly," she exclaimed, pointing out the window. "It's all downhill now. Half an hour, tops. We'll be there in time for a late lunch, I think."

There was a line-up for the ferry, which made Tim unhappy. "I'll never be allowed to drive this again if I'm not back by nightfall," he wailed. "John Coachman will have my hide."

"Don't be such a sook," Sophie told him. "If you leave without putting our bags on the ferry, I'll make sure you're the new Mrs. Vickery's personal driver. She won't put up with your whining, I promise you."

Tim had heard Mrs. Vickery. Just the thought of driving her anywhere made him shudder. "I'll carry your bags, Miss Sophie. But, I'd count it a real favour if you let me leave then," he begged.

Their turn finally came. Tim carried the luggage on and almost raced back to the carriage. He lost no time in turning around and heading back towards Sydney. Polly laughed, "If only he had driven like that when we were in the carriage, we would have been here an hour ago."

When they finally landed on the Wiseman's Ferry side of the Hawkesbury, Sophie tipped the ferryman and asked him to arrange for their bags to be taken to the inn, while Polly raced up the hill to find Mr. White. Sophie arrived as she was heading out to the stables. "I can't see him anywhere. I'm going to see if our coach is still here."

"He left half an hour ago," the ostler told them.

Half an hour ago, they had been on the other side, waiting to be taken over. If Tim had had his wits about him, he should have insisted that they went on the first ferry as foot passengers and sent their luggage across later. But, they hadn't thought about that. They'd just sat in line with the other vehicles waiting their turn.

For the first time that day, Sophie was without a plan. Polly, however, was made of sterner stuff. The north side of the Hawkesbury was her territory. "How many Wahmurra horses are here?" she asked.

"Four."

"Let's see them." When they went into the stables, she exclaimed in delight. "There's Billy's horse and the one Luc rode. Sophie, I've got a plan. Do you think you could manage to ride it?"

Sophie looked at the large grey. The more she looked, the bigger it seemed. "How far?"

"I don't know. Just as far as it takes to catch up to Mr. White. Two hours, probably. We'll leave our luggage here for the first Wahmurra person through to pick up. You and I are much of the same size. You can wear my Wahmurra clothes until it comes."

Sophie considered the alternatives. They couldn't stay at the inn. Not without great damage to their reputations. She couldn't see any way for them to go back to Sydney. Tim would be nearing Pennant Hills and wouldn't think of turning round to check on them. Billy and Luc would be in their classes. If they thought about Sophie and Polly at all, which was unlikely, they would think them safely at Mrs. Dixon's.

No. They were on their own.

"All right. I'll do it."

The ostler looked at her. "Miss Polly, I don't have a side saddle. I know you don't need one. What about your friend?"

Sophie felt horrified. She'd never ridden a horse as big as the grey, and had never ridden on a man's saddle. It was indecent, for one thing. For another, what would she do with her skirts?

"You'll be all right. Up here, lots of women use men's saddles. It's too expensive to have separate ones."

"But my skirts." Sophie said, then whispered, "People will see my legs."

"No one will care. Besides, it's practically all bush between here and Maitland. Come on, Soph. Every moment we stand here is another minute Mr. White gets ahead of us. As it is, we'll have to gallop flat out for a bit."

Sophie didn't share Polly's confidence, but she was out of her known world. "All right," she said, looking around for a mounting block. "I'm game."

She had to admit, after a mile or two, that riding a horse was infinitely easier using a man's saddle. Her sense of balance was better and she felt more in control of a horse than she ever had. It was even more than that: at times, she felt that she and the huge grey were one, and that what she thought, he did. He even sensed danger faster than she did, swerving out of the way of low branches that might have knocked her off him. He loved to race, and she was content to give him his head. They passed several drays loaded with logs, and the only time the grey flinched was when he encountered one long wagon, loaded with pigs, pulled by oxen. Sophie almost laughed as he danced his way as far as possible from their smell.

To her surprise, she enjoyed the ride and was surprised when Polly stopped and led her horse to the side of the road. "There's a good creek near here where they can drink and we can rest," she explained.

Sophie fumbled for the little watch she wore on a chain around her neck. "Polly," she exclaimed. "We've been riding for almost three hours. Where's Mr. White?"

"I don't know," Polly admitted. "He might even be behind us. There's an inn we rode around. I didn't want to stop there because ...." She broke off and held her hand out in a half-apologetic gesture.

Sophie understood. What Polly was probably saying was that the inn catered to the poorer workers who probably wouldn't know who they were and who might give them a bad time. She was suddenly grateful that Cook had packed such a huge lunch, which they'd eaten while waiting at Wiseman's Ferry. She was thirsty, though. "Where's the creek?"

Five minutes later they were set to go. "What now?" Sophie enquired.

Polly looked at her. "If you can manage to ride like you've been doing, I think we have to try to reach home on our own. I don't dare take us into Maitland. It's full of convicts and soldiers. Both could be equally dangerous. We'll try the back way. There's a little inn about two hours from here near Wallis Place. I can leave a message there for Mr. White, if he's behind us, so that he can send someone back for our bags. Then, it's only two or three more hours and we're on Wahmurra land. Are you game?"

Again, Sophie considered the alternatives. For one second. There weren't any. "I'm game."

It was harder slogging now that she knew she might be riding for another five hours. They had to pace the horses because they would be tired as well. Somehow, the dream of catching Mr. White had blinded Sophie to the various discomforts. If the grey hadn't been so well-behaved, she knew she would be aching in every muscle. Her legs and arms ached, and it was a real effort to stay awake and to concentrate on the rough road. "Let's stop," she told Polly. "I feel like I'm going to fall off."

"Soon," Polly told her. "We'll be at the inn in about fifteen minutes."

Sophie felt like crying but, of course, there was nothing she could do. Polly was in the same boat as herself, and if Polly could keep going, so could she. About twenty minutes later, Polly put up her hand to stop, then laid a finger over her mouth. "Take the horses over to the creek in there," she whispered. "I'm going to creep towards the inn, and when it's clear, run to the kitchen. I'll leave the note, have a rest, then we'll be off again."

"Can you bring some food back with you?"

"I'll try."

Polly's try was magnificent. She came into the clearing near the creek with a small basket containing cold meat pie, some cheese, bread, and a couple of apples. She even had two bottles of ginger beer.

"The cook gave us this," she said. "She knows Papa will be so grateful that he'll pay five or six times what everything's worth."

Sophie understood. She would have traded half a year's allowance for that small basket. She munched away while the horses grazed. When she looked at the sky, she frowned. "It's going to be dark soon," she observed. "Shouldn't we stay here for the night?"

"We're much safer pushing on," Polly said. "That being said, let's go. Worst comes to the worst, we'll camp in the bush as soon as we're on Wahmurra land. Then, it's another two hours to go in the morning."

It seemed a safe plan, so Sophie readily agreed. When she thought about it, they had made much better time than they had when travelling to Sydney. She hadn't realized that coaches were so slow and now she understood why Polly had felt so envious of Billy and Luc riding escort. It was much easier to ride than to sit in a carriage or coach.

Polly took them around the hamlet of Wallis Place, and Sophie was confident no one had seen them. When they crossed the bridge over the Williams River, she sighed with relief. "We're here. Now, we can rest and finish our picnic basket. Let's look for a clearing that's big enough for us and our horses, and can't be seen from the road."

They ambled on in silence. Sophie guessed the horses were exhausted and grateful for the slow pace. Finally

Polly pointed to her right. "Let's try in here. It looks like it has drinking water. There's lots of grass to make a mattress of some sort, and ferns to cover us while we sleep."

"And enough mosquitoes to bleed us to death," Sophie grumbled.

Sophie took care of the horses, brushing them down with clumps of long grass and ferns, while Polly set up their impromptu camp. "I think we've stumbled onto someone else's campsite," she said when Sophie came back. "There's a fireplace here, and over there, a shack of some kind."

"Is it dangerous?"

"I don't think so. We won't go near the shack and the fireplace looks like it hasn't been used in days. It's probably someone's abandoned house. If anyone was going to use it, they would have been here by now."

They were just settling down to eat when a rough male voice spoke from behind some trees, "Well, well. Lookee here, Dave. See what the good Lord has sent us. Two plump chickens ripe for the picking."

Two men stepped into the clearing, and Sophie's heart dropped to the bottom of her boots. She had never seen two men who looked more desperate. Not even in the middle of the rebellion in Canada. The one who seemed the leader was so filthy she could smell him right across the clearing. He carried a rifle and had a handgun tucked into his belt. His eyes looked dead with absolutely no expression.

The second man seemed different. For a second, Sophie thought she detected embarrassment and fear. He was also armed. Of the two, she knew he would be the one who had a conscience, or at least a remnant of it. She watched while he argued with the other man and felt, if there was a chance, he might listen to some sort of appeal.

Polly seemed to have some to the same conclusion. "I'm Polly Kendricks," she told the man with the dead eyes.

He grinned, a grin without any scrap of humour. "And I'm Shifty Mike and this here's Black Dave."

Sophie felt her eyes widen. Shifty Mike was the escaped convict the entire northern district was trying to catch. They had no chance.

Again, Polly seemed to read her thoughts. "Look, I don't know what you plan to do to us, but I do know that my father will give a lot of money if we're taken to him unhurt."

Mike seemed to consider it for a while. "Over here, Dave," he ordered suddenly, and when they stood on the edge of the clearing, Sophie watched while he seemed to explain some kind of plan to Dave. When Dave nodded reluctantly, she didn't know whether it was good or bad.

Mike came back to them, smiling widely and revealing black rotting teeth. "I'm going to give your father one day. One day to come up with fifty thousand pounds. If he does that, I'll think about telling him where you are. Otherwise, you won't have to look for a husband, dearie. I'll be your one and only."

Sophie felt herself trembling. Mike sounded outrageous, but she believed every word he spoke. She watched, terrified, while Dave came back from the shack and produced two long, serviceable-looking ropes.

"Now," Mike said after taking one and walking across to Polly, "let's tie you up so you don't desert me, sweet thing."

To Sophie's amazement, Polly somehow twisted herself and seemed to fly through the air feet first. She connected with Mike's private parts and he sat down abruptly, then curled into a ball. Almost at once, Dave seized her. "Run, Sophie," she yelled. "Get the horses and ride for your life."

While Dave fought with Polly, Sophie fled to the horses. She untied Polly's horse first and then the grey. She was just scrambling onto its bare back when two strong arms pulled her off.

CHAPTER 22

"We'll have none of that," Mike wheezed. "Not if you fancy living."

Sophie struggled against the iron bands that seemed to encompass her chest. "Let her go," Polly shouted from across the clearing. "It was my idea."

"That it was," Mike answered as he contemptuously threw Sophie to the ground. "And I've another score to settle with you. Tie this one up, Dave. Nice and tight, hands and feet. I'll make sure the other can't move a finger."

Dave looked half apologetically at Sophie. "Sorry, love. I've got to do it, else I'll be in the same boat as you, without a rich father to bail me out." With that, he efficiently tied her feet, then her arms together behind her back. "What next, Mike?"

Mike carried a trussed-up Polly and tossed her down next to Sophie. "Next, we try to get those horses she untied. Prime horseflesh, they were. Then, we find someone to take a message to Wahmurra. Fifty thousand by this time tomorrow and set up some kind of meeting place that's safe."

Dave added more logs to the fire. "That should hold you," he whispered, turning away from Mike. "Pull yourselves over to the fire if you get cold."

Polly turned over so that she could see Sophie. "Are you hurt?"

"Not really. How about you?"

Sophie heard a rustling sound, then Polly's voice. "I'll live. If only I could loosen the rope around my arms, we might be able to escape. It's my fault we're here."

Sophie's fingers tried to reach the knots in the rope around her wrists. "There's two of us at fault. I should have been a little faster to get on the horse. But, oh, Polly. What will we do? How can we get Dave to let us go? He's sort of kind, isn't he?"

Polly snorted. "Kind? You're saying he's kind after he tied you up? Sophie, you've got to stop thinking that all convicts are like your papa and Preacher Dan. These men are different: they're thugs."

"Dave's not a thug. He could have tied my feet much tighter. My arms are killing me," Sophie protested.

"Maybe he's a little kinder," Polly conceded. "But Sophie, neither of them has anything to lose. Mike's already shot three policemen. If the police find them, they'll hang. So, you've got to believe they're thinking, what's one more crime? After all, what's worse than hanging?"

Sophie thought back to the morning in Montreal when she had almost seen men hang, and shuddered. Those criminals had been loved and respected by at least half the crowd. From some of the other spectators though, she sensed satisfaction. They'd wanted to enjoy the spectacle of men ending their lives by dangling at the end of the hangman's rope. She hadn't understood their feelings then. Now she knew that if Mike were caught, part of her would rejoice. But, she reminded herself, Polly was right. First things first. They had to escape.

"What can we do?" she asked, wriggling around so that she could see Polly's face.

"Pretend we're asleep when they come back, for one thing," Polly answered matter-of-factly. "If they think we're harmless, they'll probably leave us alone. They don't expect a message from Papa till lunch time, at the very least. I think they'll ignore us until then."

"I hope not," Sophie said. "I'm thirsty."

Polly sighed, and Sophie sensed her frustration when she spoke sharply, "Sophie, try to understand. We want them to ignore us. We don't want them thinking about us at all. Unless, of course, you want one of them to make you his wife."

Sophie shuddered at the thought of kissing Mike, with his blackened stubs of teeth and horrible breath. "I was trying to make a joke when I said I was thirsty," she told Polly, trying to sound dignified. "Of course I want to play least-in-sight. But even if they ignore us, how can we possibly escape?"

"I don't know yet," Polly admitted. "I wish we had a knife."

Sophie pushed on her elbows and sat up. After waiting for her head to clear, she looked around the campsite. It was obviously a semi-permanent one for the bushrangers. Although the grass was green around the perimeter, it was trodden down in the centre, and almost non-existent where Mike had dumped them. With their hands bound behind their backs, they would have no hope of rifling through the men's possessions for a knife. They had a slight hope, though. Turning towards Polly she said, "There's a piece of glass or sharp tin somewhere behind me. It cut me when Dave tossed me down. Maybe it can cut our ropes. That is, if I find it."

She turned, sifting through the sandy soil with her fingers. When cramps paralyzed her right arm, she kept searching with her left hand. She heard Polly struggling to do the same, but knew she was having a harder time because Mike had tied her very tightly as a punishment for kicking him.

After about fifteen minutes of futility, she wanted to give up. Her wrists felt like raw meat. Her shoulders hurt. They weren't used to straining backwards, and she knew she had scrapes and bruises all over her legs. She shuddered to think what she looked like with her skirt rucked up to her knees and her stockings puddled around her ankles.

"Any luck?" Polly asked.

"A couple of stones that we can hold in our hands as last-resort weapons," Sophie answered.

Cheered by this semblance of hope, they renewed their efforts, shifting their bodies to better scrabble through the dirt, searching for anything to help loosen the ropes. Persistence finally paid off when something cut Sophie's fingers. "Found it," she told Polly triumphantly. "Now, if it can cut through rope the way it cut me, we'll be free in a few seconds."

"Faint hope of that," Polly told her. "But, well done. Are you all right?"

"I'm fine except for having my finger almost sliced off," Sophie answered. She grunted as she tried to cut into the rope and said several bad words when she dropped the precious shard of glass. "I've got a problem. I can't reach the rope. My fingers aren't long enough. Oh, Polly, I'm sorry. I don't think I can do it."

"Let me have a try. Hold your arms out straight. That should make it easier."

Sophie carefully put the shard into Polly's hand before twisting around so that she faced away from Polly, holding her arms as far out and straight as she could. She felt Polly's fingers on her wrists, and the piece of glass on the rope as Polly began trying to cut through it.

Although Polly worked diligently, Sophie sensed she was making no progress. Worse, the sun had set completely and she knew the men must soon return.

"We should work out how we're going to escape while we can talk," Sophie said, to take their minds off the uselessness of their efforts as much as anything. "Maybe we can take their horses."

"No hope of that," Polly told her. "They'll neigh and wicker and wake the men up. I don't think we can outrun them by using the road, either. They know this area much better than I do. This must be only one of Mike's camps." She turned her head. "There's a creek over there, to our right. I think we should go by water. I heard one of them talking about a boat before they saw us. Let's try to find it. Then, if we can just get a hundred yards or so out into the bay, we'll be safe. It's our best shot."

Sophie liked the plan. Polly had been around boats all her life. As well, she knew Port Adams. The shorter distance to safety sounded fine, as well. Neither Dave nor Mike looked like they had ever seen water, they were so filthy. It was probable that neither could swim.

The plan gave them both hope and energy. Polly resumed sawing away at the ropes and Sophie began forcing her hands apart, trying to stretch the rope as far as she could. Both were amazed when Polly cut several strands at once. Using all her strength, Sophie flexed her arms once more and a few more strands snapped.

"I think you're almost through one rope, at least," she said triumphantly.

"We're close. But it's not enough. Listen."

Sophie listened. "I can't hear anything."

"I can hear the horses," Polly told her. "They're maybe five minutes away."

Sophie had long since stopped being awed by Polly's abilities. After all, Polly had spent most of her life in the country, as opposed to the city. Her hearing hadn't been dimmed by all the din of a bustling city like London, as Sophie's had.

"Do what you can," Sophie told her, and she sat patiently while Polly hacked and thwacked at the ropes. Eventually, she, too, heard the far-off drumming sound of horses' hooves. "Okay. Stop. Leave it to me now."

"All right," Polly said. "I'll put the glass back behind me a little so we can try again when they go to sleep."

But Sophie slithered as fast as she could towards the campfire. She pushed the wood a little with her feet to get a steady flame, then took a deep breath.

"What are you doing?" Polly asked softly.

Sophie didn't bother answering. Using every ounce of courage she had, she held her wrists above the flame, trying not to scream as the fire scorched her skin.

"Sophie! Stop! It's not worth it!" Polly ordered.

Again, Sophie didn't answer as she concentrated on

forcing her arms apart. Her cheeks bulged as she bit her lips so that she wouldn't make a sound. Her eyes shut with the gargantuan effort, and even her ribs felt like they might break as she kept straining against her ropes. Against all odds, and somewhat to her surprise, she felt them suddenly give. Not all the way, but enough so that she knew she could break them later. She jerked her wrists away from the fire, moaning in relief. She didn't care how badly she'd been burnt. The knowledge that she could be free acted like a salve on the burns.

From the pounding of the horses, she judged that Dave and Mike must be cantering over the bridge leading to the clearing. As she scuttled her way back towards Polly, she whispered, "Lie on your side. I'll have to lie on my back so they don't see what we've been doing. And let's hope they're worn out and want to go to sleep quickly."

Polly's first concern, though, was Sophie. "How are your wrists? I can't believe what you did. That was one of the bravest things I've ever seen."

"Shush. They're here."

CHAPTER 23

Dave looked happy as he strode into the clearing, a dead wallaby over one shoulder, and for an instant, just before she closed her eyes, Sophie could see the man he might have been if he hadn't taken to crime.

"Well, there's another thing you were wrong about," he called back to Mike. "They're still here, still out of this world. I told you that you didn't have to hit them. Next time you'll believe me."

"Doesn't mean that you'll be right next time, though," Mike answered sourly. "One of them's stoked the fire. Wonder how she managed that if she was still out of it as you said." He grunted as he lowered an earthen jug to the ground, and Sophie knew it was ames' ace whether or not he'd come over to check on them.

"That's the other thing," Dave told him. "A pitcher of ale. Remember that I know this area like the back of my hand. Know where to get liquor, know where the rozzers hang out ..."

"Yeah. Yeah. You're a regular 'cyclopedia, I know. Well," and Sophie heard the sound of ale being poured into tin cups, "here's to ya. You gonna build the fire up more, or me?"

"I'll do it," Dave told him and Sophie heard the sounds of wood being dragged towards the firepit and, after a while, was tantalized by the smell of the wallaby roasting.

Dave tried to chatter, but Mike was absorbed in emptying the jug of ale. Dave worked around the fire, and Sophie hoped he wouldn't look at them closely. She felt her heart come to a stop when Dave announced, "It's cooked, Mike. Why don't I untie them, and let them have a share?"

Mike's voice sounded slurred as he ordered, "You keep a good eye on them, young Dave. Untie one, let her eat, then tie her up again. Then do the other. And don't give 'em the good meat, either. I want the hind legs."

Sophie tried to think of an excuse for her charred ropes, but to her relief Polly thought quickly. When Dave brought a slab of meat and a cup of water over, she said, "She's out of it. Exhausted, I think. If you leave her share, I'll give it to her when she wakes."

"Don't leave her untied," Mike shouted across the campsite.

To Sophie's relief, Dave fed Polly then put the rest of the meat in easy reach. "I'm going to have to tie you up again," and Sophie thought that, if circumstances were different, it might have been regret she detected in his voice. She felt a slight touch from Polly's foot and was reassured. *Hurry up and drink the ale*, she willed. *The sooner you get drunk and go to sleep, the sooner I can eat and get busy again on my ropes.* She wanted to sing them a lullaby. Anything that would help them sleep.

Centuries passed, it seemed, before Sophie knew she could move. Dave and Mike had been snoring for more than half an hour, and the sound didn't alter as she strained against her ropes. Daggers of pain stabbed her body, exaggerating every cut, burn, scratch, and bruise. Part of her wanted to sleep and never wake up, but fear of Mike forced such feelings aside. With a massive effort, she managed to snap the ropes, and pins and needles lanced through her newly freed arms. She flexed them gingerly as sensation flooded throughout every vein and artery.

When the pain was bearable, she sat up and began working to untie Polly's wrists. "Can you find that piece of glass?" she whispered. "It will be easier if I can cut the rope. These knots are tight."

Neither spoke while Sophie hacked and tried to slice into the rope, while Polly held her wrists apart. It was surprising how much easier it was now that Sophie could use both hands freely and, although it seemed an eternity, it took maybe an hour before the ropes around Polly's wrists snapped. "It's murder, isn't it," she said sympathetically as Polly tried to stifle her moans. "Don't worry. It will go soon. I'm going to work on my feet, then I'll help with yours."

Although splinters of moonlight gave an eerie brightness in the clearing and helped them to see better, it still took forever to get rid of the ankle ropes. Sophie almost cried in discouragement. It helped being with Polly, because they were in the same desperate situation, working towards the same goal, and able to draw courage from each other. It was perilously close to dawn, though, before they staggered towards the shore of the creek in search of the rowboat.

"I feel like a newborn foal," Polly whispered. "My legs can barely hold me up."

"I know, but hurry. I'm scared they'll wake up, and I'm too weak to run fast. I do not want to be caught again."

Again, the moon helped as they searched along the shore in its pre-dawn light. Eventually Polly pointed to a rounded hump. "That has to be it. One last bit of energy to get us into the cove proper, then we can relax and get our strength back. Oh, but I'd give anything for a drink. We should go back and steal one of their mugs."

Sophie grinned as she pulled a tin cup from the top of her dress. "Help yourself," she said blithely, pleased with Polly's look of astonishment. "I stuffed it in there thinking it might come in handy."

Polly laughed softly. "I can't believe you. I used to think you were just a spoilt city girl. Well done, Sophie."

Sophie felt her cheeks flush with pleasure. "Just for that, I'll let you drink first."

Polly dipped the mug into the swift-flowing stream. "Oh, it's so good. Nice and cold. Here. Your turn."

"Ugh," Sophie said, once she'd tasted the water. "It's salty."

"But, safe. We're lucky. Another hundred yards or so it would be too salty to be drinkable. Let's get the boat into the water. Ready?"

Once they turned the boat over, they saw that their luck was fickle. There was only one oar. "What can we do?" Sophie asked, close to despair. "Try walking after all?"

"It's too late. We can't outrun horses. I'm sorry, Sophie. It's my fault. I should have remembered that no good bushman leaves both oars with his boat. The other one's back in the camp somewhere. Come on, get in. We'll have to do the best we can."

"I can paddle," Sophie volunteered after they had pushed off and scrambled into the small boat.

Polly ignored her. "Sit towards the left," she told Sophie as she carefully made her way towards the stern. "I'm going to pole our way along the creek bed. It's not deep. But we'll have a real problem once we're into the cove. We'll have to take our chances then. I've never tried to row with one oar. Maybe we'll have to try to walk home after all."

"No," Sophie answered emphatically. She could well imagine how badly they'd be beaten if Black Dave and Shifty Mike caught them. "They won't give up, and they must know your papa will bring all kinds of help to their meeting place. If they don't have us to bargain with, they'll be killed or captured. I vote we stay with the boat. It's our best chance."

"I agree," Polly answered. "I'd much rather take our chances on the water. Anything's better than trusting ourselves to their not-so-tender mercies, isn't it?"

CHAPTER 24

Somewhat to Sophie's surprise, the rowboat reached the bay in minutes. When she tried to congratulate Polly, though, the older girl brushed her praise away. "It's the tide. It's going out. Our prayers are answered. The water's going to do most of the work for us."

Port Adams was a magnificent harbour. Sophie, of course, had only seen it from the northern side, and she was disappointed that the mist obscured almost everything. "Where's Wahmurra?" she asked.

"Over there," Polly answered, pointing northwest. "Even if there wasn't a mist, you couldn't see it from here because of the islands. But, the mist is good for one thing. If we can get just a bit further out, Dave and Mike won't be able to see us because of it. Then, we can rest while the boat drifts and let the tide carry us."

"Great. I'm so tired I can hardly keep my eyes open."

But it wasn't as easy as they thought. Instead of heading towards open water, the boat wanted to wash its way along the shoreline and it resisted Polly's attempts to push it into deeper water. "Give me the oar," Sophie demanded softly. "Hurry. We don't have time to argue. I think Dave and Mike have discovered that we've escaped."

Indeed, the noise of a tremendous ruckus could be easily heard. "It's the water," Polly explained as she handed over the oar. "It always seems to amplify sound, especially as it's so early. She settled herself in the back of the boat. "What on earth are you doing? I thought you'd try to row," she asked, a puzzled look on her face.

"Paddling," Sophie said, standing precariously in the front of the boat, working the oar first on one side, then the other. "It won't be fast, but it will help put more distance between us and them."

"Looks like really hard work," Polly said. "It's effective, though."

"I wish this boat was one of the canoes we had in Abbotsford. This is tiring, and I won't be able to keep it up for long. Just long enough to get us away from shore, I hope. Then, as you said, we can rest." She paddled on, her strokes becoming increasingly slower as she tired.

"Can you go faster," Polly whispered. "I can hear someone splashing behind us. I hope he can't swim."

From her higher vantage point, Sophie could see one of the men dog-paddling in the shallow water near the shore. "It's Dave, I think. I hope." She almost overbalanced as she thrust the oar into the water with a renewed sense of urgency. "Right, two three. Left, two three," she began chanting, hoping that the rhythm would help her.

She was so tired that she had to take a rest after a couple of minutes. When she looked back, Polly had unlaced her boots, taken off her stockings and was pulling her dress over her head. "Polly," she gasped, "what are you doing?"

"There's no public here. It's just you," Polly said as she stripped her petticoat off as well. "I don't have time for Miss Prim's Rules of Propriety. I'm getting into the water and I'm going to push from behind. You just keep steering us out towards that island, Soph."

Sophie immediately stopped paddling. But even as she did, she felt the boat begin to move forward and saw a steady splashing where she imagined Polly's feet might be. Encouraged, she resumed paddling and, as she began chanting again, she noticed that Polly's splashing kept the same rhythm. Better yet, they began to put a sizeable distance between them and whichever man was dog-paddling after them.

Still, it was nip and tuck. Although Sophie wanted to die from exhaustion, the island came steadily nearer and soon the waves' momentum pulled them towards it. "Can you see a safe place to land?" Polly called weakly.

"I think so. There's a small beach to our left. Are you all right?"

"Tired. Can you still see whoever's coming after us?"

"It's too choppy."

More by luck than good management, Sophie managed to "catch" a wave, so that it carried them onto the beach. Polly waded towards shore, looking very bedraggled in her shift and underdrawers. Sophie pulled off her boots and stockings, jumped into the water, and started tugging the boat onto the sand.

"Wait," Polly told her. "Run up the beach a little more. See if whoever it is has given up."

Sophie ran about twenty-five yards inland and, from the higher vantage point, saw a black head bobbing up and down in the waves. "I think it's Dave," she called back. "He doesn't seem to be coming after us, though. I don't know what he's doing. He doesn't seem to be going anywhere. Maybe he'll turn round and go back."

"Fat chance. You take our things above the high-tide mark while I hide the boat in the rock pool over there." She pointed to a spot about twenty yards along the beach where a mass of vines overhanging the water and a jumble of moss-covered rocks would shelter the boat from prying eyes.

While Polly pushed the boat back into the water, Sophie carried their clothing and the precious tin cup higher up the beach. Deciding to look for a safe place for them to sleep, she pushed her way through the tall grass and fat-leaved purple pig-face only to stop as she heard a blood-curdling scream.

"Polly? What's wrong?" she yelled as she ran back to the water's edge. Polly bobbed up and down in the water and seemed to be in tremendous pain. "What's happened?" Sophie asked as she began wading towards her.

"Don't come closer," Polly shouted. "There are oysters everywhere. When I jumped from the boat, I landed on them. My feet feel like they've been cut through to the bone."

Sophie thought for a moment. "Can you swim across to me? I'll wrap your feet so that you don't get sand in the cuts."

She pulled her dress over her head. It had enough holes it in that she didn't needed superhuman strength to tear two large strips from it. With them in hand, she waded into the water. The waves had carried Polly until she was just a few yards offshore, with the water around her becoming redder and redder.

"Hurry, in case there are sharks around," she gasped. "They can sense blood from enormous distances and I'd rather not be their dinner. Sand in my feet is better than that."

Sophie clumsily tied the strips around Polly's feet, shuddering when she saw the bloody mess. The cuts looked deep and oozed blood. "Can you walk?"

"I'll try."

When Polly tried, though, she collapsed. "Can you drag me?"

Sophie grunted and groaned as she tugged her friend from the beach, and her arms felt like they were being pulled from their sockets. When she stopped for breath, Polly slid on her bottom, and with Sophie helping her over some rough spots, they eventually reached a little clearing about fifty yards from the beach. Banksia bushes and gum trees provided shade, yet there was also a sunshine-flooded space where they could dry their clothes.

"Let's stay here for a while," Sophie gasped after she had made Polly as comfortable as she could. "Are you in much pain?"

Polly didn't bother answering. She wriggled until she was half in and half out of the sun, moaned quietly, and buried her head in her arms. Sophie ripped two more strips from her dress and replaced the wet bandages with the dry ones. Then she lay next to Polly, enjoying the sun's warmth on her body until she fell asleep. But almost immediately, or so it seemed, Polly prodded her. "Sophie! Wake up! Listen!"

"Oh, go away. I can't hear anything."

"Wake up, Sophie."

Sophie forced her eyes open and strained to hear. At first she heard nothing. Then she jerked upright at the sound of a man weakly shouting for help. "Oh, no!"

"Has to be Black Dave. What will we do?"

CHAPTER 25

Sophie ran to the beach and came back slowly. "It's him. About seventy yards out. He's going to drown if we don't help."

"How can we? I can't get to the boat. You can't swim well yet, so it's dangerous for you to go out there. In any case, how do we know he won't do something horrible to us?"

"We don't," Sophie said. "But we can't let him drown. It would be like murdering him."

"Yes, but we don't want him murdering us, do we?"

That was unanswerable. "I have to try," Sophie said. "I'll take the boat and see if he can hang onto it. I won't get in the water, and I'll bash him over the head if he tries anything."

Polly looked at Sophie, with a sort of embarrassed look on her face. "Do you pray?"

Sophie stared in amazement. "Of course I do. In church, and before I go to sleep. Don't you?"

"Let's ask God to protect us. You're showing the 'greater love' that Jesus talked about. You know. 'Greater love hath no man than he should lay down his life for a friend.' Surely God will honour that."

"I hope so," Sophie answered. "I don't mind the greater love bit, but I really don't want to lay down my life. Let's hurry."

Polly grinned, and somewhat to Sophie's surprise, prayed simply, as though God was in the little clearing with them. Sophie barely waited for her "Amen" before she raced for the beach. "There's rope in the little storage locker. Use that if you have to. Don't forget to put your shoes on," Polly called after her.

"Yes, Mama," Sophie muttered, but she nevertheless grabbed her boots and shoved her feet into them once she reached the rocks. Carefully, she stepped into the boat and pushed it off with the oar. When the water became too deep for poling, she got the rope from the locker then carefully walked to the front of the boat. Dave's cries for help were fainter now and she only saw his head occasionally because of the waves. "I'm coming," she yelled every now and then to give him hope.

Paddling against the tide was extremely hard work. Her arms ached, and she kept telling herself that it would be easier going back. "Paddle, two, three," she chanted, because, somehow, the chant's cadence numbed the

241

pain. Caught up in the rhythm of her strokes, she forgot to keep track of Dave and paddled past him. Anxiously, she scanned the water and felt relieved when she caught sight of his terrified face. "Hold on," she yelled. "I'm going to circle back."

"Help me," he said weakly.

"I'm trying to, aren't I?" she told him, paddling vigorously. He looked in desperate shape as the waves washed relentlessly over him, and for the first time Sophie knew there was a very real possibility that one of them would drown. Even when she reached him, she didn't know if she could save him. "Can you grab hold of a rope if I throw it to you?"

"I think so," he muttered through chattering teeth.

Sophie knotted one end of the rope to the seat behind her and tossed the rest of it towards him. It fell short. "Of course. Why did I ever think this was possible?" Sophie muttered as she reeled the rope back for another try. "Hang on. Let's have another shot at this," she told Dave. "Can you catch it?"

"I'll try. I've got a terrible cramp, though."

"Keep your mouth closed and your head out of the water," she told him. This time the rope almost touched him. He grabbed it, and immediately went under with the effort. She could see him struggle to surface. She wanted to jump overboard as Polly would have done, but then two of them would have needed rescue. To her relief, he surfaced and trod water feebly. "Can you climb in?"

Dave tried but fell back into the water. "I'm as useless as a new-born kangaroo," he told her. "Useless. Good for nothing. That's me."

"Tie the rope around yourself," Sophie told him. "Can you do that?"

Dave tried, then gave up and simply wrapped it around his hand several times. "If this doesn't work out, make sure you save yourself. I know I don't deserve this."

"Now you tell me," Sophie said half under her breath. If she had wanted to save herself, she wouldn't have been on the water in the first place. The best thing she could do was to get him to the shore as fast as she could. She dug the oar into the water with renewed determination and, as if it sensed her thoughts, the boat fairly danced its way along the waves.

"Almost there," she called out encouragingly, but there was no answer from Dave. When they reached shore, again the momentum helped, because the boat almost deposited itself high on the beach. Sophie jumped out and grimaced when her boots filled with sand.

Dave lay half in and half out of the water, his face a peculiar colour. "Don't you dare die on me now," she exclaimed, tugging him further up the beach. "Not after I went out there again."

There was no answer. "I'm back, but I think he drowned," she called to Polly.

She heard the scuffling sound of bushes being pried

apart, then Polly answered, "Open his mouth, then turn him over on his stomach."

Muttering to herself, Sophie did what she was told. "How does that help?"

"Put his hands on top of his head so that his elbows stick out sideways." Polly waited a few seconds before she asked, "Have you done that?"

"Yes, ma'am."

"Now, kneel so that one knee is on either side of him at about his waist."

Grumbling, Sophie clambered over Dave's body then dropped to her knees. "Now what?"

"Spread your fingers apart and put your hands on his ribs. Then, you go, push, two, three. Push, two, three. About six times. Then lift his elbows. Try to work them like a bellows. You're trying to get air into his lungs."

It sounded simple but, of course, it wasn't. She pushed and counted, then lifted Dave's elbows and counted, then repeated the sequence. "What's happening?" Polly called.

"Nothing."

"Keep trying." There were the sounds of bushes breaking, Polly's muffled yelps of pain, then slithering sounds as Polly worked her way to the beach on her bottom. When she arrived, Sophie realized that the effort must have opened her cuts, because the bandages were strained bright red.

"Here's what we're going to do," Polly said matter-of-factly, as though there was nothing wrong with her. "Turn him over, but keep his elbows the way they are. This time, when you push on his chest, I'll lift them. Ready?" After about five minutes, Polly put up her hands. "All right. Rest a little. There's one more thing. It's rather horrible, but I've seen a sailor do it. Once. It worked, though."

While Sophie watched in horrified fascination, Polly held Dave's nose shut with her fingers, then opened his mouth and breathed into it. Sophie could see her counting as she did so. Without asking, she reached for Dave's elbows, and timing her motion with Polly's count, began lifting them. She felt, rather than saw, the result.

Suddenly, Dave's chest heaved. Polly screamed, "Look out," and scrambled out of the way as he vomited sea water. He coughed a couple of times but kept breathing on his own.

"We've done it," Sophie said, her aches and pains temporarily forgotten.

"Yes, we have," Polly said, her voice echoing Sophie's triumph. "But what are we going to do with him?"

"Do unto others ...," Sophie began.

Polly laughed. "I don't think it means that we should tie him up just because he tied us up."

"But it's the best solution, isn't it? We have to get you settled again, and I feel like I could sleep forever. Neither of us can guard him as we are right now. I don't know how long it will take him to recover. He must have swum more than a mile, then almost drowned. If he wakes up and feels like us, he'll sleep the clock round. So, I say we tie him up."

"You're right," Polly admitted before dragging herself back to the campsite. "Do you have enough energy left to drag him into the shade?"

"Just. Then I'll try to clean up your feet."

Sophie pulled Dave's arms behind him, tied his wrists, tugged him fifteen yards or so to a small patch of native grass. She used fern fronds to make him a pillow, and knotted the sodden rope to a tree. Satisfied that he was safe from the midday sun, she trudged her way along the beach to Polly. She had the uncomfortable sensation of being watched. A couple of times she stopped and looked around, wondering if there were aboriginals on the small island. Somewhat fearfully, she looked across the water to where she imagined Dave and Mike's campsite might be, but saw nothing.

Even while she changed the bandages on Polly's feet, she couldn't shake the feeling that she'd missed something or somebody. That sense of being watched had been so strong.

Chapter 26

Sometime later, Sophie woke to the sounds of Polly muttering and thrashing about in her sleep. Immediately, she put her hand on the older girl's forehead. "You're so hot," she told her. "You must have had too much sun."

However, she knew it was something worse. Polly had grown up in New South Wales and was accustomed to its sun. If anyone were to have the sunstroke, it would be Sophie herself, not Polly. She stared at her friend with increasing concern. Water, she decided. Maybe wet cloths could keep Polly cool while Sophie searched for fresh water.

She ran back to the beach, found the pile of discarded bandages, then tiptoed carefully to the shaded rock pools. After soaking the cloths for several minutes, she took them, dripping wet, back to the clearing and placed them across Polly's forehead and neck. That done, she found the tin mug and tried to imagine there might be drinkable water.

They had landed on the southwest side of the island. A large hill, running north to south, divided it. If she climbed the hill, she'd not only be able to see exactly where they were, but she should encounter at least one stream running down towards the sea. Or so she hoped.

Clambering over rocks, Sophie pushed her way through some dense underbrush and realized the island had to be larger than she thought. Every now and then she disturbed birds sucking nectar from pink bottlebrushes and red waratahs. Distinguishable by their bright green and red feathers, lorikeets flashed about in the treetops, chattering their displeasure at the human intruder. After a while she had a sense of real climbing, and she was grateful for the years she'd spent on her beloved Mount Donne in Vermont. At least she could still do one thing well in this upside-down world of New South Wales.

When she heard the sound of running water, she turned towards it. A small stream splashed over rocks, tumbling its precipitous way towards the bay. Sophie couldn't reach it fast enough. After greedily downing two or three mugfuls, she wondered if there was anything better to drink on earth. But how could she get more than a mugful at a time to Polly and Dave? Wearily she resumed climbing, keeping her eyes skinned for something to carry water in until, fifteen minutes later, she reached the highest point of the island.

The view was panoramic. She looked back first, to see where she'd come from. The bay, which had seemed so big, was nothing but a tiny cove. She thought she could see the rowboat above the high-water mark, but knew it could be a shadow of some kind. When she looked northwest, her heart skipped at the sight of a cluster of buildings nestled against low hills. Wahmurra. There were even a couple of ocean-going ships anchored in its harbour. For a moment, she thought about making a beacon, but realized that Mike might be able to see it as easily as the captains on those ships.

She could well imagine the activity at Wahmurra. Lord Peter would have galvanized the whole place into a bustling maelstrom once the news of their capture reached him. She wondered how well Lord Peter knew his daughter, and if he knew she'd do her best to escape and try to reach Wahmurra by water. She thought he'd probably concentrate his efforts on finding Mike's camp and not even spare a thought about the possibility of them being marooned on an island in the bay. As she pondered his thoughts and emotions, she was glad that Papa and Lady Theo would not have reached Wahmurra yet. Unaware of events, they would not be worrying. If possible, she was even gladder that Luc and Billy were at King William's. If they knew, they would have ridden off, half-cocked, and got in everyone's way.

When she turned east, the sun's light was hard and bright. With her back against a gnarled tree, she squinted into the distance. Large brown cliffs guarded the entrance to Port Adams and she could see a ship tacking its way through the heads. Irrationally, she wondered if it might be the sloop bringing Papa and Lady Theo back, but decided the odds were against that.

Islands of various sizes dotted the harbour and, when she looked back to the northwest again, she began plotting her route to Wahmurra. Seven islands lay between her and Polly's home, and she thought she could use them as stepping stones. She could paddle as far as the third, rest, get fresh water, then go on to the fifth. If she made good time, she might even be able to do the trip in one day. The only problem was: would Polly survive long without drinking water?

At least she knew how they could escape and where the best route was, Sophie thought as she began scrambling her way down the hill. Her search for something like a jug had been unsuccessful and when she reached the stream again, she drank her fill and began searching anew for something to carry water. It was more by luck than anything that she finally found part of a stump in the creek itself. It was unwieldy but it had the advantage of being so waterlogged that it retained water. Holding it carefully, she resumed her downward path.

When she reached the camp, she took a mugful of water from the stump and held it against Polly's mouth.

Polly woke, gulped the water down, and asked for more. Sophie gave her a second cup and Polly collapsed back onto her bed of ferns. After picking up some of the discarded rag-bandages, Sophie walked down the beach towards Dave. It would be too bad if he died of thirst after the effort she and Polly had gone through to save him. She sighed when she thought of the work entailed in supplying both him and Polly with water. Being a rescuer was a lot more trouble than she'd ever imagined.

After putting the rags and her petticoat into the rock pool to soak, Sophie trudged along the beach, kicking a path through dried seaweed. When she looked to where she'd left Dave, she froze. He wasn't there!

Chapter 27

Panicking, Sophie ran the short distance. She saw the rope, neatly coiled, and Dave standing against the tree. While he whittled away at a piece of wood with a penknife, he watched warily as she walked towards him.

What a fool she'd been. She hadn't even thought to look for a weapon in his pockets. She kicked a pile of seaweed in frustration, then spun round and raced back to the rock pool for the oar. If he tried to capture her, she'd do her best to beat him off with it. He'd have the knife, but the oar's reach was longer. When she looked back, she saw him standing halfway between the tree and the rocks, his arms open, and his hands outspread in a gesture of defencelessness.

"I'm sorry I frightened you," he said in his surprisingly educated voice. "I won't hurt you. I'm too grateful. You've saved me. Twice."

"Twice?" Sophie asked in almost a squeak. She stood with the oar clenched in both hands while she tried to assess his sincerity.

"Twice. Once from drowning, and once from Mike."

"From Mike? I didn't save you from Mike," Sophie said in disbelief. "We saved ourselves from Mike."

"And in doing so, you showed me that I, too, could escape from him. I decided that I didn't have to be with him. Maybe there is a way to get my troubles sorted out. I'm not really a lawbreaker, you know. I'd much rather live on the islands by myself than go back to be with him."

Sophie heard the words, but didn't believe them. She stood still, not knowing what else to do. If she dropped the oar, she'd be defenceless. On the other hand, she couldn't stand there all day. "How do I know if I can believe you?" she eventually asked.

Dave kept his distance, and they faced each other like wary cats, neither willing to give an inch. "I can cook a meal for us and find water," he eventually said.

Sophie thought that she'd have Buckley's chance of getting him tied up again. "Could you? Bring water, that is. I found a creek, but it's halfway up the hill. I brought some down in a mug for Polly and I was going to go back for some for you. But you're only one worry. I think Polly's running a fever."

"Would you trust me to find out?"

Sophie looked at Dave in astonishment. He was cleaner than she'd ever seen him, and he certainly appeared less threatening. Maybe, just maybe, he meant what he said. Meant that he was truly grateful for not drowning, and willing to help them. "What can you do?" she asked half-skeptically.

"Back in England, my mother was the village healer."

Sophie shrugged. She didn't know what that meant, but it was better than anything she could offer. She had almost no experience in sick rooms, and absolutely none in diagnosing illness. Polly's flushed cheeks and overly bright eyes didn't look normal, but how could she tell? Dave certainly had been in New South Wales long enough to have seen victims of sunstroke. What would she lose by taking a chance? With Polly ill, they were at his mercy anyway. "Come on, then," she said ungraciously, and began walking towards the clearing. "Should I take the wet cloths with me?"

"Can't hurt."

She trudged up the beach behind Dave, cloths in one hand, the oar in the other. When they reached Polly, she seemed to be unconscious. After a fast look at her, Dave dropped to his knees. He gently put his fingers on Polly's forehead, then whipped them away as though he'd been scalded. "She's running a fever all right. Get those wet cloths on her forehead and tell me what that's all about," he ordered, pointing to Polly's bandaged feet.

"She jumped onto an oyster bed," Sophie answered. "We were trying to hide the boat from you."

Dave ignored the gibe and whistled after he unwrapped the bandages. "There's her problem. Oyster shells are nasty things. Full of infections. We've got to get her fever down. That's the first priority."

Sophie rolled her eyes. Just what did he think she'd been trying to do? "What can we do except put wet cloths on her?"

"Where was this stream you found?"

"Up there. Halfway along."

"Did you follow it down to see where it went into the bay?"

"I didn't have time. I was too busy trying to work out how to carry water down for both of you."

Again, Dave ignored the gibe. He walked around the clearing, muttering to himself. "I think we should try to find a better place," he said eventually. "Somewhere closer to running water. It will make nursing her easier. Do you want to come with me or stay here?"

"If I stay here, I can keep her cool," Sophie said.

"But, you'll be able to bring more drinking water if you come with me."

Sophie gestured towards the path. "Lead on."

CHAPTER 28

Dave set a fast pace, and Sophie found it difficult to keep up with him. "Do you know where we are?" she asked, hoping he'd slow down.

"No Goat Island."

Sophie grinned. She never ceased to be amused by the strange names in New South Wales. Deadman Creek, Blackfella Billabong, and Mary's Revenge, to name just a few.

When Dave's pace didn't slow, she collapsed onto a log. "Dave. Stop. Please. I have to rest."

Dave came back and looked at her searchingly. "We can rest for a while. I forgot you'd be exhausted." However, he remained in motion, pulling bark from trees and smelling it, and carefully gathering some weeds. To Sophie's astonishment, he began examining every tree and shrub in the area.

"What are you doing?" she asked.

"Getting supplies." He took off his shirt and carefully put the weeds in it, then made it into a bundle by tying the sleeves together. "Are you ready now? You can go back to Polly, if you'd prefer."

"No, I'll go on."

Dave found a long stick in the undergrowth and pushed it through the shirt bundle. "Can you carry this over your shoulder? It's not heavy. Just make sure it doesn't touch you."

"Why? What's in it?" Sophie reached for the stick and swung the bundle over her shoulder. When Dave told her that the weeds were stinging nettles, she almost dropped them. "Why are we carrying them?"

"I want to find out where the stream goes. We probably won't come down this way," he answered.

"I meant, why do we need stinging nettles?" Sophie asked.

"They'll fight the infection. It's native medicine."

"Oh. I guess that makes sense. They don't have doctors, do they?"

"They have their own doctors," Dave replied sternly. "Don't underestimate them, Miss Sophie. They know things we don't. They can follow a man for miles and miles simply by looking at the ground he walked on. And we're going to carry a lot more water than a mugful back to Polly by using one of their tricks. Ah, here's your stream. Do you need another rest?" he asked, filling the mug and bringing it to her to drink.

"That tastes good. Thank you. And just a short rest, if you don't mind." She sat on a mossy log by the creek and trailed her hands in the water. "Would you tell me about No Goat Island? How did it get its name?"

Dave laughed and, for a moment, Sophie forgot her underlying fear of him. "Oh, some fellow heard a rumour that there was a herd of goats here. When he came to look, he saw a couple of them on the beach and paid a fortune for the island. Of course, as soon as he went away, the man who sold it to him collected his goats and took them back to his farm. Anyway, the story spread like wildfire, because no one likes the man who was fooled. Everyone knows about it. It's gone up to Taree, over to Maitland. It's probably down in Sydney. I tell you, Miss Sophie, if ever anyone needed to be separated from his money, this was the man." He smiled at the memory of what had obviously been a very good joke. "Anyway, enough of that. Let's start back."

They followed the creek, with Dave pulling strips of bark off a few trees. Sophie knew he must have some purpose, but she decided not to ask. He'd made her feel foolish, and she didn't care for the experience. So, they clambered over rocks and were almost at sea level when Dave exclaimed in satisfaction, "This will do. It's a better campsite. Close to the stream, close to the sea, yet sheltered. There's even an old fire site."

The clearing they had come to looked much the same as the other one to Sophie's untrained eye. "How will we get Polly here?"

"I'll carry her. Here's my knife. You get a bed ready for her then start collecting dry wood. After we get her settled, I'll try to catch our dinner. I made some fish spears while I was waiting for you to come back."

Using Dave's knife, Sophie cut ferns for Polly's bed and arranged them near a clump of flannel flowers. They reminded her of small sunflowers except that their "flowers" were a greyish-green. That done, she scoured the area for sticks and old branches so that Dave could build a campfire.

It took much longer than Sophie expected before Dave reappeared with Polly slung over his shoulders. "She's heavy," he grunted, while gently lowering her onto the fern bed. "I think her fever's worse. Undo her bandages while I find a couple of stones to smash these nettles into a pulp."

"There," he said in satisfaction minutes later after he'd covered Polly's lacerated feet with his pulpy mess. "That should help."

"Won't the nettles sting her?"

"Strangely enough, no. I don't understand how it works, but the nettles seem to cancel out the pain while they bring the infection down. I'll make her some nettle tea as well, once we get the fire going. That will help bring her fever down."

Sophie looked around the campsite. "How are you going to boil water? I can't see a pot."

"Ah. That's where this comes in," he answered, pointing to the pile of bark. "These strips are from paper bark trees. I'll soak them in the stream until they're waterlogged and make two or three containers. If you'll give me the laces from your boots, I'll tie them around each end so that they'll hold water without it running out."

"But won't my laces burn?"

Dave gave her a pained look. "They won't have time to. You'll see." He took some sheets of the paper bark and deftly molded them into bowls. He walked to the stream and came back carrying water in one of them. "I'm off to catch fish. Want to come?"

Sophie shook her head. "I'll stay with Polly. She'll be frightened if she wakes up and doesn't know where she is. Is there anything else I should be doing?"

After he'd gone, Sophie lifted Polly's head and made her sip a little water from the mug. Then she gently lowered her again to the bed, hugged her knees to her chest, and began to think. Obviously, they couldn't go on like this. She or Dave would have to go for help. Dave might be able to get across to Wahmurra faster, but he would have a difficult time convincing anyone there that he had Polly's best interests at heart. Everyone would see him as a kidnapper, and if he wasn't shot on sight, he might be too badly beaten to talk.

She didn't know what to make of him. He had been wonderful today. Resourceful, and his knowledge of the bush was already having a good effect on Polly. Sophie would never have thought of using stinging nettles. She wouldn't have known how to catch fish without a fishing rod, nor could she have worked out how to carry water by using paper bark.

But Dave was also the Dave of yesterday. A terrifying bushranger who had kidnapped them, tied them up, and only barely restrained Mike from hurting them further. He had seemed to be frightened of Mike, although she had to admit, he had gone along with almost everything Mike had suggested.

Why had it seemed that he'd given up on everything? Given up on being believed, and on ever getting justice? Maybe he had told her the truth. That their escape and refusal to be held prisoner had spurred his own escape. If so, things had changed. If she could trust him, she wouldn't have to worry about Polly when she went for help tomorrow.

Just after dawn the following morning, following the route she and Dave had worked out, Sophie climbed into the boat. As the tide was going out, she used its strength to help her paddle northeast from No Goat Island. The first stage was longer than she would have planned by herself, but it took advantage of the tide. She was relatively well provisioned with leftover fish, some nuts, and a bark container full of water. As she didn't have to stop for water when she became thirsty, she was about halfway to Wahmurra when she stopped for a rest on Derrigo Island.

Dave had made the trip easier in another way. He'd used the firelight to whittle a makeshift paddle for her. When she left Derrigo, she found the water choppier than she was used to. However, she consoled herself that all the time she spent listening to Barney talk about wind and tides when she was learning to sail would help her now.

She wondered what Dave would do when the rescue boats came. Would he fade into the bush and watch while the men from Wahmurra took Polly to safety? Or, would he decide to take his chances? He'd gone outside the law by becoming a bushranger, and certainly had no right to expect justice. Sophie had tried to tell him about Lord Peter Kendrick. Even though Lord Peter was a magistrate, she was sure that he would listen to Dave's story with an open mind. If not, maybe she, Luc, and Billy could help him escape.

Here and There Island was the last island on her route, and when she rounded its tip and hit open water, she let herself relax. Her hard work had paid off. She tossed her head and the breeze whipped through her curls. She knew she looked a mess, but she didn't care.

Ordinarily, she would have only half an hour to paddle. But, because of her exhaustion, she thought she had only one more hour. Then, boats would be on their way to Polly, and, she prayed, she would get the medicine she needed in time.

Just that thought renewed her sense of energy. Telling herself that she could rest later, she drove the paddle into the water with renewed determination. She would do everything she could to get to Wahmurra in time for Polly to be rescued that very night.

To distract herself from the pain that seemed throughout her body, Sophie thought about Luc and the many adventures they'd had. How silly she had been when she'd pined for another. How incredibly young, for she now knew the cost of a life and death adventure. She would never forgive herself if Polly died. Never.

She wondered if Luc ever thought that way, or if males had a different way of looking at things. Just a couple of days ago, Luc and Billy had been talking about going to England together. They would probably have to do another year of school before they could go on to university. It had sounded so funny to hear Luc, who had tried to evade school for the entire time Sophie had known him, talking about Eton as a grand adventure.

She had accepted the fact that Luc would go away in the next year or so. Marc was insisting on it, and Sophie knew how strongly Marc influenced his brother. It was only because Luc wanted to please Marc that he'd become involved in the rebellion in the first place. Sophie still had nightmares when she thought what would have happened to her if Luc hadn't come to her rescue so many times.

Well, she could do something to repay her debt. She could finally face the fact that she was married, that the strange ceremony in Montreal was legal throughout the British Empire. Papa had explained some of its ramifications to her, although he had stressed that it would be years before it became a problem for Luc and her. But did Luc want to go to England shackled to a girl half the world away? She doubted it.

When Papa and Lady Theo came back from their honeymoon, Sophie resolved that she would tell them to get her marriage annulled. Papa had explained it one night. An annulment meant that in the eyes of the law, she and Luc would never have married. Both of them would then be free to marry whomever they wanted.

Tears poured down her face as she realized that one part of her belonged to Luc. He had always been her safety, her anchor if anything had gone terribly wrong. Only now, when she was able to free him, did Sophie realize just how much she loved him.

While she thought, she had paddled without paying attention to the conditions around her. When she looked up, she realized with relief that she had paddled straight, and that Wahmurra's wharf was only a thousand yards or so away. Once again, she was tempted to relax, but snapped to attention when a voice she knew shouted from just behind her, "There she is, mates. I told you we'd catch her."

Mike!

For several long seconds, Sophie froze. She heard the words but was unable to believe the evidence of her ears. Mike should not have been anywhere near Wahmurra. If he were caught, he'd be hanged. The best possible outcome for him would be Norfolk Island, a notorious island prison.

Then she shook her head and dug the paddle feverishly into the water. No murderer was going to keep her from getting help for Polly. One of the anchored ships looked to be only five hundred yards away. If she could race Mike to it, she'd be safe.

Paddle, two, three, she chanted to herself. Paddle, two, three. Paddle, two three. She couldn't feel pain in her shoulders anymore. The blisters on her hands were forgotten, the splinters didn't hurt. Every atom of energy was concentrated on pushing the boat through the water.

When she looked back to see if she'd gained any distance, she groaned in despair. Mike's boat was only fifty yards away and, worse, the tide seemed to be pushing her towards it. That didn't make sense, though. The tide was coming in, not going out. She and Dave had plotted the times so carefully. But, no matter how hard she paddled, she seemed to be going backward. When she lifted her paddle out of the water, the boat increased its speed. It seemed to have a mind of its own. Then she remembered a story Billy had told that night over the campfire a year before.

He'd said that a convict boy, Thad, had almost drowned because he'd got caught in an underwater current. According to Billy, there was something called a "rip" a couple of hundred yards from the Wahmurra wharf. It was so strong that it could take boats a mile or two off course. Sometimes, Billy said, it even carried them right out to sea. She had to be caught in it, she decided, but remembered there was a way to break free of it. "You have to go at an angle," Billy had said, slanting his hand in the firelight as he explained. "You can't go directly against it. You have to go sideways across it."

Sophie looked back at Mike's boat. The men seemed to be caught in the rip as well. She could see them rowing with all their might, their shoulders straining, but their boat seemed to be going nowhere. If Billy's advice worked, she'd have a chance.

She paddled furiously on one side of the boat, forcing it into an angle, and even though it seemed that it took two strokes instead of one to make progress, she eventually saw the gap between her and Mike's boat increasing. The men rowing it seemed not to have worked out their problem, or else they didn't know how to counteract it.

Finally, when she dug hard into the water, and the boat spun around backwards, she knew she was free of the current. Now, she felt every single ache and pain as she paddled slowly towards the wharf. "Help," she shouted as soon as she was in earshot. "Help!"

A sailor on the ocean liner spotted her first, and a dinghy set off from his ship. But her cries had also been heard at Wahmurra's wharf, and as she was towed towards it, she saw people running down from the House and Barracks.

She was so tired she couldn't stand up, and had to be carried up the dock's steps. "Polly," she kept saying. "Got to get help for Polly. No Goat Island. Lady Peter has to go."

When Mr. White appeared, the chaos disappeared. He listened to Sophie's story and immediately sent for Lady Peter. "Don't fret, Sophie. You've done your best. We'll get her back here tonight."

Lady Peter came running down the hill, her bag of medicines in her hand. She knelt and swiftly examined Sophie. "Make sure she drinks a lot. Get her into a cool room and put a salve on those hands of hers. I'll dress them properly when I get back," she told the housekeeper who had rushed to the wharf.

"Hurry up, Lady Peter," Mr. White called out. "We're going to need every moment of daylight."

As soon as Lady Peter stepped aboard Wahmurra's new steamboat, it set off towards No Goat Island. Mr. White then sent three boats, full of armed men, out into the bay. There was much discussion about how far they'd have to row to find Mike. It wasn't a question of if, Sophie realized. The men were confident that they'd not only find Mike's boat, but be able to bring him back to justice. "He'd be better off if he simply jumped overboard, and saved us the trouble of bringing him back," one grumbled as he set off.

Mr. White carried Sophie up to the house himself. There, she found hot water already in a bath and the housekeeper waiting to help her into it. "I've added some special salts that her ladyship gets from England," she told Sophie. "You just lie there, dearie. There's more hot water when you're ready."

Sophie yelped when she first got into the bath. The pain in her hands was unbearable. But, as the rest of her welcomed the soothing water, she lay back with only her hands and face out of it. The housekeeper clucked when she saw Sophie's raw, blistered hands and wrists, and later as she smoothed salve over Sophie's burns, she told her a little about what Wahmurra had gone through in the past twenty-four hours.

Everyone had known long before Mike's message had reached them that something was wrong. Once Sophie had untied them, the horses had headed for home. Mr. White saw them on the road, recognized them, and had thought that Billy and Luc could be in trouble. He'd organized search parties. The man Mike had forced to take his message had been intercepted almost immediately, and the search had changed to one for Sophie and Polly.

"Lord Peter was prepared to pay the ransom," the housekeeper confided as she helped Sophie into her nightgown. He rode to the place he was supposed to meet Mike, but that dastard wasn't there. Of course, we now know why. Lady Peter said all along you two would escape."

As soon as she climbed into bed, Sophie closed her eyes. She could find out what happened tomorrow. After saying another brief prayer for Polly, she fell asleep.

CHAPTER 29

On a cold winter's day in June 1844, Sophie and Polly took the *Sophronia* out for a special sail in the harbour, just off Double Bay. "It feels good to be young again," Sophie said.

"Young! You're not old," Polly immediately rebutted.

"Sometimes I feel decades older than seventeen," Sophie said, holding a hand over her eyes and looking back towards Sydney. "I can't see a ship yet."

Polly shrugged, and immediately Sophie was reminded of Luc. Two years earlier, she and Polly had also been in the *Sophronia*, waving goodbye to him and Billy as they set sail for England. In the last letter she received, Luc had written that, although they both loved Oxford, they missed Sydney. Luc thought that strange. He had expected to be homesick for Montreal. "But, then, Montreal doesn't have you," he'd finished.

Sometimes, the waiting for Luc and Billy to come back seemed an eternity. But Sophie had adjusted, somewhat, to enjoying life without Luc. As the wind hurled a wave's spray against her face, she shivered. "I suppose we should have gone into Sydney with Papa and Mama and said goodbye in person."

Polly wiped seawater from her own face. "It would have been the civilized thing," she agreed, albeit with a grin.

"And we're just so civilized," Sophie laughed. "Hey, look! There's the *Achilles* now. Where are our signs?"

As the *Sophronia* bobbed up and down, they stood holding their signs as high as possible as the HMS *Achilles* sailed slowly into view. Dozens of men crowded the deck, and once they spotted the *Sophronia*, they cheered and waved.

"There's Mr. Lepailleur," Sophie shouted, almost jumping up and down. "*Bon voyage. Bon voyage.*"

"Goodbye, *mes braves*," Polly yelled. "Goodbye."

Sophie and Polly stayed on the water, waving, until the *Achilles* passed through the heads, taking most of the Canadians away from what Lepailleur called "the land of a thousand sorrows." As Polly expertly set the sails for home, Sophie reflected on the men she had known, to some extent, for nearly six years.

They were honest men who had fought for their families and homes. Many, she had found out, hadn't understood the politics of the rebellion. All they had seen was a dangerous threat to their way of life. They had been outstanding citizens in Sydney and would be missed. Unlike other convicts, they had thrived financially because their families had meant so much to them. If they had not been pardoned, and thus allowed to sail off in the *Achilles*, they would have been able to pay for their wives and children to come to Sydney.

But then, on the other hand, it was their families and parishes who had worked ceaselessly for their full pardons. Sophie well remembered the wild celebration once the first of those reached Sydney. There had been a party at Meillon's Inn in Brickfield Hill. Sophie thought she'd never forget its exuberance because Benjamin and Lady Theo had danced on top of the tables. Sophie smiled at that memory, while she expertly tied the *Sophronia*'s ropes to stanchions on their wharf.

"I'll miss them," Papa said the following afternoon. "They taught me a lot. Particularly, how important a family is."

"That's good, dear," Lady Theo said as she handed one-year-old Michael to his father. "You can entertain him while I dress for the Governor's reception."

"Don't worry, Papa," Sophie laughed. "I'll take him."

Sophie sat in the bay window, staring out at the harbour. Papa was a free man again, thanks to the pardon he'd received from Queen Victoria. He, Lady

Theo, and their investors in England had bought half a million acres just north of Wahmurra. Black Dave, now a free man, was its resident healer, and once again, Papa ran a lumber company.

She wondered how his old company was doing in Malloryville. Had her brothers sent it into bankruptcy? Probably. Would they ever meet young Michael? Probably not. Would they care about that? No.

Would she ever again know the happiness and uncertainties of the past few years? Sophie hoped so. She didn't like bland or ordinary. Her life, so far, had been exciting and full of adventures. Surely adventures wouldn't stop because she had grown up. She couldn't imagine Luc without the glint in his eye that signaled something unusual for them to pursue, and she hoped she never lost her eagerness to be with him.

Almost fifty years after the Achilles *sailed out of Sydney Harbour, a newspaper, the* Echo, *published a series of articles on the history of various areas in the city. Sophie, Luc, Lady Theo, and the Kendricks weren't mentioned, because they're entirely fictional. Surprisingly, however, the Canadians were still remembered, although they had been in Sydney for such a short time. This quotation from the article on Macdonaldtown tells what the Canadians did, and more importantly, what they were remembered for fifty years later:*

Some touching stories are told by old residents of their care for the poor in the neighbourhood where they were at work. Many of them kept an informal sort of night school. There was such a school at Paddington, where a party of the Canadians were employed quarrying stone for the Victoria Barracks. There was another in Macdonaldtown while they were there, and there were others wherever gangs of them were employed in making the Parramatta or other roads. Wherever they were at work, they earned the respect and gratitude of their neighbours, and when they received their free pardons and were allowed to return to their native country, they were

greatly missed by the poor of Sydney and
the suburbs.

That legacy is incredible. It's hard to imagine any other group of convicts setting up schools, giving money to the poor, doctoring the sick, and being "greatly missed." Canadians everywhere should be proud of the men transported to Sydney.

A Historical Note and Acknowledgements

When I was young, I spent most of my holidays at a place called Tahlee. On the north shore of Port Stephens, about one hundred and fifty miles from Sydney, Australia, it had been the original residence for the owner/manager of the Australian Land Company — a huge estate of five hundred thousand acres. Traces of its glorious (and inglorious) past were everywhere. The floor of the ballroom, for example, had no nails in it. Convicts, guarded by soldiers, had built it. For a while — from its heyday in the 1830s and 1840s to the late nineteenth century — it had been a place where the powerful and well-connected vacationed.

In my time, Tahlee was owned by Mr. White. I remember him as a very kind person who gave me fountain pens to help me write my stories down on paper. I hope he would be pleased to find a version of him and his estate in this book.

Many people helped with my research. The archivists and librarians of the State Library of New South Wales were extraordinarily helpful. So were Betty Stanbury and the various Tahlee Ministries people I met while staying at the present-day Tahlee. My cousin Dr. Margaret Sharpe (who is nothing like the Mrs. Sharpe in the book) vetted the aboriginal details and researched details about Sydney's operas and music in the early 1840s. I am much indebted to The King's School of Parramatta, N.S.W. and its archivist, Jenny Pearce, who so patiently answered my questions. Peter and Diane Cunningham provided a Sydney base and much support.

I also thank my Vancouver friends who proofread or critiqued the manuscript: Melanie Anastasiou, Chris Greenwood, Paul O'Rourke, Susan Pieters, Irena Tippett, Bronwyn Short, Kathy Tyers, Gordon Wilson. Barry Jowett, the editor, did his customary great job.

FACT OR FICTION?

The Mallorys, Kendricks, Thornleighs and Morisets are entirely fictional, although Marc Moriset is based on Jean-Marie-Léon Ducharme and Benjamin Mallory on Benjamin Mott. Port Adams is also fictional. The King's School of Parramatta, established in 1831, is my inspiration for King William's College.

The Canadian convicts spent almost two years in the stockade farm at Longbottom. Their activities, particularly the illegal businesses at night, are factual. The most striking thing about them was their desire to be reunited with their families. Their diaries — the only ones known in convict history — were written because they intended to share their experiences with their families. The most detailed of these is the one kept by Maurice Lepailleur, *Land of a Thousand Sorrows*, edited and translated by F. Murray Greenwood. Basile Roy, who couldn't read or write, paid Lepailleur to keep one for him as well. The history of the Canadians' stay in Sydney can be read in my own book, *A Deep Sense of Wrong*, published by Dundurn in 1995.

The Bath Arms is still in existence. When you're older, you might live to visit Sydney and stop in at the Arms. As you drink your beverage, remember the men who lived across the way from it, in the area now called The City of Canada Bay.

I hope you enjoyed meeting the Kendricks family. Many of its secrets are revealed in my next two books. I enjoy hearing from my readers. Find my web page and follow the links to send a message to me, or else write to me care of my publisher:

The Dundurn Group
3 Church Street, Suite 500
Toronto, Ontario, M5E 1M2.

Lastly, I thank the Canada Council for the Arts for the literary grant which supported me during the writing of *Sophie's Exile*.